What Michael Saw

A Spiritual Warfare Adventure

By Catherine Key

Blessings to you!

Catherine Key

The Armor of God

Finally, be strong in the Lord and in his mighty power. Put on the full armor of God, so that you can take your stand against the devil's schemes. For our struggle is not against flesh and blood, but against the rulers, against the authorities, against the powers of this dark world and against the spiritual forces of evil in the heavenly realms. Therefore put on the full armor of God, so that when the day of evil comes, you may be able to stand your ground, and after you have done everything, to stand. Stand firm then, with the belt of truth buckled around your waist, with the breastplate of righteousness in place, and with your feet fitted with the readiness that comes from the gospel of peace. In addition to all this, take up the shield of faith with which you can extinguish all the flaming arrows of the evil one. Take the helmet of salvation and the sword of the Spirit, which is the word of God. And pray in the Spirit on all occasions with all kinds of prayers and requests. With this in mind, be alert and always keep on praying for all the saints. Ephesians 6: 10-18

God's Warning Against Witchcraft

Let no one be found among you who sacrifices his son or daughter in the fire, who practices divination or sorcery, interprets omens, engages in witchcraft, or casts spells, or who is a medium or spiritist or who consults the dead. Anyone who does these things is detestable to the Lord, and because of these detestable practices the Lord your God will drive out those nations before you. You must be blameless before the Lord Your God. Deuteronomy 18:10-13

Prologue

Willy lay on the desert floor, his motorcycle in ruins, twisted handlebars and bent metallic components of his Harley all around him. The truck that had run him off the road was a dark smudge on the horizon. The driver never stopped to find out what happened to him. "Typical of my whole life," Willy gasped in pain. His fingers were wrapped around the neck of his shattered guitar, the essence of all that he treasured on this earth.

Suddenly the shimmering blue sky above Willy was filled with angels and demons doing battle. He recognized most of the demons. After all, Willy had lived with them. There were demons of drugs and alcohol, demons of lust and greed and largest and most powerful of all was the demon of selfishness that had caused Willy to abandon his family nearly a decade ago. Willy felt the life begin to ooze from him. Despite the fear of death tormenting his mind and pain racking his body, the battle scene transfixed Willy. This vision of a spectacular battle being waged in the heavens just above him was clearly a battle for his very soul.

A massive and brilliantly clad angel cut a swath through the dark angels. He swung his sword with power and grace. The dark demon that was speaking to Willy was pale and his touch made Willy's arm go cold and numb "You are hopeless. Give it up and come with me!" The Champion of God swung his mighty sword and knocked the demon Hades from Willy's side. "The battle is not over, Enemy! Leave us!" The angel's voice rang with authority and power. Then the Warrior of God stung the enemy agent with the tip of his mighty blade and sent him cowering behind a pillar of orange rocks.

"Look at me Willy, do you remember me?" Willy looked right into the angel's eyes and saw love and hope looking back. His eyes focused on the angel's rugged face. "Benedict? Is that you?" The angel replied as he knelt and held Willy's crumpled form in his strong arms. "Yes, it's me!" "What are you doin' here, man? I thought I set you up with money for supper and a bed to sleep in last night at the Done Inn," Willy whispered. He was incredulous at the improbability of it all. Last night Benedict was a street bum he had shared a meal with. He had given him some extra cash from a gig that had been very lucrative. He liked Benedict, with his sense of humor and easy charm. Most of all he liked the fact that Benedict saw something good in him. Not too many people had seen any virtue in Willy…only his wife and kid…possibly his mother.

"The Good Book says to be kind to strangers, Willy, because you never know when you are entertaining an angel in disguise." Benedict smiled at the fractured man he held to his heart.

"You an angel? Can you get me out of this one, man? Like can you save me or something?" Benedict breathed grace onto Willy's upturned face and his dimming vision cleared for a moment.

"This is your time to step into the eternal, Willy, but I do know Someone who can save you and give you life everlasting. The best part is that it's a free gift!"

Despite the fearsome message Benedict had just given him, Willy managed a weak smile. Somehow Benedict's presence gave Willey courage and the glimmer of hope, "If it's free, I'm listening!" Benedict poured out the story of Salvation to Willy. He spoke of Jesus' merciful mission to earth. He detailed Christ's life of loving example lived in poverty yet brimming with power. Benedict's voice broke with emotion as he told how Jesus, by dying a criminal's death on a cross, took upon Himself the just punishment for the sins of the world. The gift of a restored relationship with God was Willy's, if he but confessed his need as a sinner and opened his heart to Jesus as his Savior and Lord.

In the dying moments of the day, a God of mercy empowered Benedict's words with grace. Willy listened to Benedict intently with a hunger for a new life that was burning deep in his heart. As the sun set crimson stains on the bleak desert sands just outside Las Vegas, a man who had been claimed by the Enemy turned his life over to Christ. Cheers rose into the sky as God's Champion Benedict ascended to heaven carrying his new friend Willy like a wonderful trophy to present at the throne of the Lord. Willy, for his part, was weeping with joy trying to take in all the beauty of his new home. Best of all was the ecstasy of love and joy that was pouring into his long forsaken heart. "Benedict, I can't say thanks enough for what you've done for me! You are Awesome!"

Benedict, the mighty warrior of God, looked a bit timid and shy at the compliment. "For me, the best part of my job is seeing a lost soul won for my Lord. As surely as I enjoy doing battle with the enemy, it's nothing compared to seeing peace replace fear in your eyes, Willy!" The man hugged the angel in speechless gratitude for all that he had done.

After several seconds of silence Willy looked a bit sheepishly at Benedict. "You've already done so much for me, I shouldn't ask more of you. Can you do one last favor for me? Can you look after my son? I left him with my ma nearly ten years ago. She's a good woman, but a boy needs a man to guide him. I realize that now."

The angel turned toward the throne. "We'll ask the Master what should be done. He always knows what's best!" Benedict set his new friend down and clapped Willy on the back. "Jesus wants to have a word with you and welcome you into His Kingdom!" Willy was drawn into the arms of Christ, where he received the love he had always sought and answers that filled him with peace.

CHAPTER 1

One special night in the present age of this world in a small town in the Midwest known as Bridgeton, children were being snuggled into their beds by parents. Prayers were said, blankets tucked in and kisses bestowed.

The heavens gleamed with particular beauty. Trails of light, like streaking comets shimmered in the sky. This light was not ordinary, but of heavenly origin marking the descent of the Holy Spirit to God's children. It was an evening to dream dreams that come from the throne room of God.

Michael was one of a dozen young people who received a special dream about Jesus that night. He lay in his twin bed gazing out the window at the light streaked sky. "Mom, did you notice how the sky is lit-up tonight? Isn't it unusual?" Michael questioned.

His mother peered out the window and commented thoughtfully, "It looks like a display of the aurora borealis. It doesn't usually travel this far south. Maybe this extremely cold weather from Canada brought it in. I'll have to check the late news to see if anyone comments about it!" Michael's mother ruffled his hair and felt his forehead. "I'd say your fever is gone. You feel very cool to the touch. Get comfy under those blankets and get a good night sleep!" Mom doused the lights and blew Michael a kiss, returning downstairs where the T.V. set droned in the background.

As he pulled his multi-colored comforter up to his chin Michael was aware that the soft wheeze that had accompanied his seven-day episode with the flu had suddenly gone.

"No more fever and you sound a lot better, young man, so back to school with you tomorrow," were the goodnight tidings his dad had left with him before he shut the door to the small bedroom. Actually, Michael was slightly bored with the cartoons and soap operas and was secretly glad to be returning to Ms. Adam's fifth grade class in the morning.

While he lay there waiting for sleep to overtake him, Michael started thinking about the homework assignment that his friend Brad had given him over the phone.

"It's about that book Ms. Adam's started reading to us after lunch recess. You've missed the last three chapters, but I think you can do this one anyway. We're supposed to write about Chad Charmer as a hero and how we could be more like him in our daily lives. We get bonus points if we write our own magic spell at the conclusion of our paper," Brad had advised.

Brad was the best student in the class and Michael had no doubt at all that he would probably be going for the bonus points.

"I did the best I could writing about Chad, that was the easy part," thought Michael. "That stuff about writing my own spell, every time I would pick up my pen to write I just couldn't get into it! When I went to do it I got this cold feeling in the pit of my stomach and my mind just went blank. Maybe I'm not as recovered as Dad thinks I am."

As usual, Michael spent his last few minutes in prayer before drifting off to sleep. He prayed for his family, his friends and his school. He prayed about problems facing him in class. At last Michael sank into slumber. Although he was unaware of it, a holy light filtered into his room and surrounded Michael with a golden glow. The radiant light was most pronounced around Michael's head making a halo that spilled onto his pillow. This holy light, which was a miraculous sign of the presence of the Holy Spirit, intensified on Michael's eyelids.

A soft voice murmured like the sound of rushing water, "Blessed are you to see what you shall see, Michael, for I shall give you anointed sight." Suddenly Michael experienced warmth flowing through his body that settled him into a deep and peaceful rest. Projected onto his closed eyelids was a vivid image of Jesus. He was smiling and extending a hand toward Michael.

CHAPTER 2

"**M**y children, come sit at my feet." The invitation was spoken softly yet Michael felt the urgency in Jesus' voice. Into a fragrant heavenly garden streamed a dozen boys and girls from near and far. Although there were twelve vying for position, there seemed to be plenty of room to nestle at the feet of Christ.

Michael sank into a cloud-like bank of grass and wondered to himself if he were dreaming or if this was really happening. Never had he experienced a dream so detailed and clear. He could see Jesus' nail-scarred hands; the wounds looked deep and fresh. Compassion rose in Michael's heart, and a fresh wave of devotion broke over him like a mild electric thrill.

Jesus' eyes grew more serious and sorrowful. He spoke quietly but firmly. "I am calling you to be prayer warriors in the Great Army of God. You shall not be the least or smallest in this army. Because of your great faith and trust in me your prayers shall be mighty weapons in the great battle taking place on earth."

Michael felt wonderfully close to Jesus, even though there were many other kids with him. How blessed and important this moment was! How could Jesus use kids like me? Michael wondered.

With a sweep of His hand, Jesus cleared aside some of the grassy growth beside the flat rock on which He sat. A vision of the earth appeared and the children leaned forward with eyes wide ready to see what Jesus would show them.

The earth appeared like a beautiful blue and green jewel suspended in space. White clouds swirled just above the surface of the shining sphere. Suddenly a dark cloud appeared and spread, at first slowly and then taking on speed it consumed the earth. The black cloud was alive with wicked voices and mocking laughter.

Jesus spoke, "Dear children, this is the earth as I see it without the love and prayers of ones like you. Satan, the enemy, and his demon army are spreading hatred and lies everywhere. Do not be afraid because I am with you. I will lead my army and your numbers will grow. There is a great harvest of souls in the world waiting to be set free from this darkness. They are crying out for freedom and for the light of my truth."

Jesus turned his gaze to the globe at His side. Great beams of red and white light poured from His heart. "This is my mercy and grace," Jesus whispered. Answering beams of pure light shot out from the darkness. Angels of God encircled the globe fanning away the dark clouds here and there. The angels shouted encouragement and cheered as new beams of light winked on everywhere.

"The light you see comes from grace received and used by my prayer warriors. They are responding to my call as you children are doing now," Jesus explained.

Through the clouds that had parted the group could see the earth zooming in closer and closer until the visions' perspective was just a few feet above ground level. From this vantage point they could see young and old alike dressed in golden armor. They had great swords in their hands and wherever the swords swept, ugly demons ran for cover. People who were chained to these beasts were set free as the swords came down and broke each chain apart. Some of the chains were woven with links that spelled out words like, " jealousy," or " prejudice." Others were woven with spiked metal that said, "idolatry," or "witchcraft," or "hatred."

Soldiers, strong and bold, were clad in armor that shone with the name of Jesus. Their golden swords fell against the thick black chains again and again. Single blows freed some slaves; others required sustained efforts by many of Jesus' troops.

The group cried out in one voice as some captives were carried off to dark caves and recesses in the earth before the golden army could free them. Michael felt his cheeks dampen with tears. He recognized some of the prisoners in this scene. They were classmates and teachers that he knew well at school.

Many captives seemed unaware that they were in bondage, and yet they responded to every hideous claw that yanked them here and there, until they stumbled into dark pits.

These pits were guarded over by large demons wearing ebony crowns. Written on the crowns in dark glowing jewels were names of sins, lies and calamities. Some of the largest demons on the battlefield were wearing crowns emblazoned with certain sins: idolatry, witchcraft and blasphemy.

One group of these dark phantoms played with videotapes, books and games for children. They smirked and laughed aloud as they fingered through one of the most popular book series for kids that celebrated involvement in witchcraft and wizardry.

A foul-breathed demon with bulging eyes much like a toad's wheezed in delight, "Let's lift a toast to the New York Times best seller's list. I hear this one's become a movie with several sequels in the works!"

In one of the demon's claws was a poisonous brew sloshing over the edge of a tarnished goblet. The other scaly arm held aloft a thick volume, the cover of which featured children cloaked in black, encircling a cauldron.

Suddenly a strong beam of light caused them to cower and flee. Several children aged nine or ten were holding hands in a schoolyard, their heads bowed in prayer. They were dressed in golden armor and were encircled by angels lifting huge shields.

Michael was astonished to see this group of five girls and guys. He recognized them as his casual friends. Sometimes Michael ate lunch with Raffi and Bobby. They always said a quiet grace before meals, which impressed Michael as very sincere and unusual. Michael's skin prickled with excitement.

He lifted his face toward the Lord's gentle smile and questions flowed from his heart, "Dear Jesus, I know these kids. They are in my class. How did they get these awesome angel guards? When were they given the golden armor? Where did the swords come from? I think I need all of these things too. I want to help them win whatever battle they are about to fight! Can you use me, Lord?"

Jesus replied tenderly, "Each of you has a guardian angel assigned to protect you and to offer encouragement and wisdom. The golden armor is given upon request to those who wish to join my army of spiritual warriors."

Michael appeared puzzled, "Do you mean all we have to do is pray on this armor and it appears?"

Jesus' eyes sparkled as he spoke, "My book, the Bible, tells you to pray for the complete armor of God in order to take a stand against the enemy and not give up." The other children leaned in closer to Jesus to hear every word He said.

Jesus addressed all the children, " This is not magic or imagination. It's very real armor. It's so simple to ask Father God for it, and He is eager to give it to you. We have a vast supply in heaven and not enough warriors are enlisting and using it. The armor consists of putting on My Presence and trusting in Me for victory. I have already defeated the enemy at the cross two thousand years ago. You need to remind him of that defeat! Everything that you need is in Me. Just stay close to Me, trust in Me, and believe in Me!

Michael saw that the vision was fading. The last thing he focused on were the swords of different sizes flashing from the military belts each "soldier" wore. "Jesus, what about the swords? Why are some of the swords more powerful than others, Lord?" Jesus answered, " The swords are carrying MY WORD. If you read my word and learn it you will have a mighty weapon to wield against the enemy. You can make your weapons more and more powerful as you learn my Word in your Bibles! Then you can use it against the enemy. I advise you not to go into battle with a toothpick at your side!"

Michael laughed, but he knew Jesus was serious. "But, Lord, Why do you need prayer warriors? Isn't Father God the boss? Isn't He and aren't You and the Holy Spirit like infinitely more powerful than Satan and his devils?" Michael asked with a keen interest to understand how prayer could effect the outcome of battles on earth.

"Michael, you are right, God is infinitely more powerful than the enemy. It has to do with a deal God made in the beginning of human history. The deal was with Adam and Eve. God made them and their offspring the boss of the earth. They had authority over everything that was made there. God also gave them free will. Satan tricked Adam and Eve into sinning, trusting in him over God. The tragic truth is that they handed over the authority for the earth to the powers of darkness. The just judgment of sin is death and eternal separation from God. That is why I came to earth as a human, Michael. I had to destroy the works of the devil and restore your relationship with God. I did this on the cross when I took the punishment due all of mankind. I give the gift of salvation to those who look to me as their Savior and choose to follow Me. My Authority is given to those that trust in me and believe in my death and resurrection. It's like having a power of attorney, Michael. You can ask your mom to explain how that works. Prayer releases God's grace and work on earth. I provided the Victory, but people need to use it. Every believer has a vast resource from Me. That's where prayer comes in. God wants people to turn to Him, ask Him, and trust Him. Someday soon I will return and throw Satan into the fiery abyss forever. His days are numbered, my friend, and he knows that. Until then, there is much to be done! I am so proud of you, Michael for having a willing heart. You will win battles for the kingdom because of your faith in Me!" Jesus embraced Michael.

Michael felt that he could remain in this peaceful and perfect garden with Jesus forever. He murmured in his sleep, "This is so strange because I know that I am dreaming this, yet I wish that it were real. I wish that I could stay here! Although I know that I must return home, there is a battle going on out there that I have to join. "

Michael's ability to focus on images in the dream grew dim. It was as if a bank of clouds were enveloping him. Jesus rested his hand on Michael's shoulder and said, "I am sending you forth, young warrior! Remember all I have taught you tonight. I am with you always!" The last thing Michael would remember was the powerful love that shone from the deep blue eyes of the Lord.

Chapter 3

A white light filtered into Michael's room, but it was no longer starlight. "Hey, Michael, get up! Rise and shine for a wonderful Wednesday at George Washington Elementary!" Michael rubbed his eyes and focused on the bespectacled and smiling face of his father hovering above him. There was a clump of shaving cream just under his Dad's left ear and it made Michael laugh. His Dad, who was a bit of an absent-minded professor, was probably wearing one navy and one black sock to boot. Michael focused toward the floor to see if he was right.

Mirth rose in Michael's throat as he suggested, "Hey, Dad, you might want to check out the laundry basket again to see if there is another pair of navy and black socks in it!"

"Never mind me, lazybones, haul yourself out of the rack and get ready for school or you'll be lining up for class in your p.j.'s!" dad retorted. Michael rolled out of bed and headed for the bath room. Several minutes into his morning routine Michael froze stock-still toothbrush in hand. As he pondered his reflection in the steam-fogged mirror, Michael experienced a sudden flashback of his vivid dream vision. It rolled through his mind like a video, with all the clarity and reality that he had experienced the night before. Michael must have stood there for a good ten minutes before he heard the familiar sound of his mother calling him to breakfast.

"Hurry, or your eggs will get cold!" Michael threw on the pair of jeans he had worn yesterday and his favorite navy shirt with "Bears," emblazoned across his chest then flew down the steps taking the last several in one bound. Although his legs were working double time, his mind rolled into slow motion wondering about the import of his dream. "Was God trying to communicate with me while I was sleeping?" Michael wondered. "What a strange dream! It felt so real and I remember it all. Usually I only remember pieces of my dreams, and then they are so weird I can't make sense of them."

"Hey, kiddo, slow down and chew some of that bagel. It's difficult to swallow those things whole," joked his dad.

"Michael, I watched the late news and weather and aside for the snow that's expected at the end of the week, there was not one mention of any meteorological phenomenon of any kind. No UFO's sighted or meteor showers reported. I really think that was an aurora borealis we saw last night. I'm surprised Channel 6 didn't pick up on it, aren't you?" Michael's mother was slathering cream cheese on her bagel then layering on the scrambled egg and adding cream to her coffee.

"Mom, I was wondering, what does 'power of attorney' mean?" Michael asked as he remembered more details from his dream.

"Well, that means you can sign and enforce contracts for someone else, like in their absence. If a person trusts you to have that power, you have the ability to act on their behalf. You can draw on their bank account, sign checks; you have access to their wealth and power, Michael. It's a position of great responsibility. You give this power to someone you really trust. Usually it's a close relative or a spouse. Why do you ask?" Michael's mother was pleased that he was interested enough in her work as a legal secretary to ask that question.

Michael was blown away with this bit of information, "Wow, Awesome!" was all he could say because he was thinking about how that might work between Jesus and himself.

"You never answered my question about what you thought the lights in the sky were last night. Any insights? You're always on the net, what's the scoop?" his mother was chattering as she filled her thermal mug with coffee for the ride to work.

"Mom, I'm not sure about last night at all. We've got to talk about it later, but right now I've got to head out or I'll be late for school!" Michael was barely intelligible with a mouth full of breakfast. Gulping down his orange juice and a vitamin thrust into his hand by dad, Michael rushed out the door barely taking time to shove both arms through the puffy sleeves of his down filled jacket. A blast of Arctic air convinced him to take the time to zip up the front and to yank the stocking hat out of his pocket and pull it on.

With eager strides Michael walked a short five blocks to school passing by the beginning of the shopping district. He took note of the Christmas decorations that were beginning to appear in windows of the bookstore he passed and smiled at the fat Santa doll in the town toy store display case. Even Sally's Bakery featured a display of sugar cookies cut out in traditional holiday shapes and frosted with green and red icing. The stationary store was the last commercial building on the route to school, and what Michael saw in that window caused him to stop short.

"I can't believe this! It's like someone is trying to mix Halloween with Christmas. It gives me the creeps!" Michael mumbled aloud. For a good five minutes Michael stood and took stock of the Chad Charmer Christmas ornaments which included Chad on his famous broomstick Bronco, a black cauldron filled with holly and marked with the words 'Christmas Spells,' as well as a glittering snowy owl sporting a wizard's cap and golden glasses. Michael had been both intrigued and repelled by the Chad Charmer book his teacher had begun to read aloud to the class.

"That owl is Chad's familiar," Ms. Adams had explained. "The term 'familiar' means that the animal has been possessed by a spirit sent to guide Chad in his exploits in witchcraft," Ms. Adams had taught. Michael remembered the lesson quite well.

All at once, Michael was aware of a dark half human, half animal form within the store hovering over the display. Its face was almost like that of a man, but twisted horns sprouted from its forehead like those of an exotic breed of goat. Looking into its crazed eyes made Michael shiver all over. Suddenly the dark form merged with the owl ornament. The owl's eyes locked with Michael's and sent a message, "Beware of me!" The pure malicious hatred exuding from the creature's eyes was palpable and hung like a poisonous vapor in the air. The razor-like beak of the owl opened and Michael could somehow hear not the usual hooting call of an owl, but mocking laughter that made his stomach churn with revulsion and fear. The chill wind was a mild tropic breeze compared to the cold blast that went right to Michael's bones.

"Dear Jesus, be with me!" Michael whispered a short prayer of protection. In the blink of an eye, the demonic aspect of the owl vanished from sight. "I know that I saw that little devil!" Michael spoke aloud, yet he questioned what he saw and tried to dismiss it.

"Thanks a lot, pal...I like you too!" replied Frank Fenelli. A smiling reflection of a fellow fifth grader appeared in the window above Michael's own serious face. Michael spun around while his classmate Frank grabbed onto his arm and yanked him along the sidewalk. "Come on. We're going to miss the bell!" Frank was a good friend and the best athlete in school. Michael, a good three inches shorter than his buddy, jogged along side and did his best to keep up until at last they were in the schoolyard of G.W.

Everyone from Ms. Adams class had already filed into the room, so Frank and Michael were last to appear. "Do you have a written excuse for your absence, young man?" Ms. Adams queried. Michael opened up his backpack and rummaged around until he found the note written hastily on one of his Mother's floral note cards.

"Here it is. I'm all over my sore throat now," announced Michael presenting the note. Ms. Adams backed up a bit, but stretched out her arm and snatched the excuse from Michael with two fingers, as if it contained all the germs which had made Michael miss two days of school.

"Line up for gym, would you please? And don't forget to bring along your art supplies because the gym teacher will be bringing you directly to art after gym class." Ms. Adams was glad for the long early to mid-morning break, which allowed her to breeze out to Dipping Donuts and grab her morning requirement of cappuccino and two glazed donuts. The shop was just one block north of the elementary school, but the wind-whipped tree outside the classroom window gave her second thoughts about leaving the warmth of the room.

"What do you think, kids, do I have time to get some donut dunkers for you guys?" The question was met with an affirmative cheer that was unanimous.

When the students returned from gym and art classes, some still sweaty and tired despite the cold, a more cheerful Ms. Adams greeted them. She had been sipping a steaming cup of her favorite blend and from the stack of bags and boxes piled next to her desk, had accomplished some holiday shopping. "I'm so pleased I had time to buy my holiday cards while you were at your specials," she shared this bit of information conspiratorially with the class. Michael smiled but the smile froze on his face as Ms. Adams stepped away from her desk revealing the snowy owl ornament he had seen that very morning in the shop window. Michael was quite sure there was some entity winking malevolently from the large dark eyes of the owl. The wings glittered with white sparkles representing a dusting of snow on the outstretched fringes of each span.

"Ohhhh, isn't that ornament absolutely gorgeous," enthused Fawn Wainwright. Fawn, a/k/a Moonbeam, along with her two older sisters and both parents, were devotees of Wicca, the practice of nature worship and "white" witchcraft. It was not surprising that she admired the owl since many of her notebooks had owls or sleek cats doodled upon them.

"Yes, I thought that this ornament would add a touch of atmosphere to our featured reading this afternoon. We'll save the little donuts for that time as well because I don't want to ruin your appetites for lunch!" Michael shivered as if from a cold draft. He turned toward the back of the room to see if a window had been left ajar. He saw with great consternation the cause of the chill. Perched on the bookshelf in the rear of the room was an ugly horned demon cloaked in white robes that shimmered as if touched with snow. Atop its wrinkled brow was a purple wizard's cap spangled with golden stars. As their eyes locked, Michael realized they were the same cruelly malicious eyes he saw peering from the owl a moment ago. As a matter of fact, Michael was more than certain that it was the very same demon he had encountered in the shop window much earlier that morning.

"Jesus, help me! Am I losing my mind?" Michael lowered his head and rubbed his eyes as if to clear his vision. When he looked up Michael was so startled that he completely forgot about the demon. There standing beside him was the most amazing angel Michael had ever imagined. The angel looked masculine, powerful and huge, but a kind and comforting light shone from his eyes.

The angel bent low and whispered into Michael's ear. "Don't be afraid. The Lord has sent me to guard over you. My name is Benedict and you may call on me at any time. You are not at all crazy, Michael. The Lord wants to reassure you that He has given you a gift. You were present with the Lord in a special way last night during your dream. He has sent you forward into battle as a guide, a scout if you will. You are blessed with the ability to see into the spirit realm. You will witness great battles and be able to guide others with wisdom because of what you can see and understand. I am with you, always by your side. Remember that!"

With a flash of light the angel, as well as the demon, vanished from Michael's sight. Michael sat still as a statue on the edge of his chair. As if to complete the resemblance to a sculpted figurine, Michael's face had taken on the pallor of white marble. His mouth was open and his breathing was fast and shallow.

"Michael, did you hear what I asked you about the South Pole region? I asked if you knew from your reading if it was an arid or moist climate? Are you all right? You look pretty pale and shaky there, guy!" Ms. Adams was almost kind in her questioning, but there was an edge of nervousness in her voice. "If you are going to get sick, please excuse yourself to the bathroom, Michael!" she continued.

Almost with a sigh of relief, Michael answered Ms. Adams, "I'm fine, it must be the bug I'm recovering from. I'm sure that I read that the South Polar Region is like a desert. There is under an inch of precipitation annually, but it accumulates to great thickness because the temperature never allows for melting." Michael was glad to relate to the natural world for a moment and was pleased that he knew the answer to Ms. Adam's question.

"Good for you, Michael, that's correct. Scientists in the South Pole regions have taken some of the coldest temperatures ever recorded on this planet. As you know, and as we discussed last week, there are no native people who live in the most southern continent. Unlike the North Pole where there are many native peoples, the South Pole is just too cold and inhospitable for any variety of land mammals to exist, including the human species. Scientists have to wear specially designed clothing to venture outside their polar laboratories for even the briefest periods of time. It is so cold there that flesh can freeze in just a matter of seconds."

Michael considered this information and found it fascinating. He enjoyed geography more than almost any other subject taught by Ms. Adams. He loved learning about the diversity and natural wonders of the planet and even believed that his future was somehow tied to this interest, which also included a keen curiosity about archeology. Michael secretly imagined himself to be an explorer like Ernest Shackleton, Captain of the Endurance. In the past year or so most of his daydreams featured himself as leader of a great and daring expedition into the wilds of the Antarctic, to the heights of the Himalayas or to the colorful netherworld of the coral reefs of Australia.

"Let's finish this morning up by silently reading the next two chapters in our text. They center on the animals, which do manage to survive the rigorous climate of Antarctica. I want you to especially concentrate on information about the whales and penguins. There are some questions I want you to answer at the close of each chapter. Write your responses and keep them in your polar folders. We will discuss these questions tomorrow," Ms. Adams advised. Michael happily threw himself into this work, half hoping in his heart that the visions he had seen this morning were temporary figments of his imagination, or at worst, the left over hallucinations from his past feverish condition.

After finishing the assigned reading and writing Michael allowed himself time to reflect on the strange happenings of the morning. "That angel I saw and heard was awesome! Could it be possible that I will continue seeing this stuff? Dear God, it IS pretty exciting, but I don't want to be weird, or act crazy because of it. Why is this happening to me?"

The last half of what Michael thought was directed as a prayer, and the response came swiftly. "This is Benedict. You can only hear my voice right now, but I am telling you that your gift will make you different. It sets you apart from others, Michael, but it will be for your good and the good of others. You will understand more about this gift as time goes on. In the meantime trust in the Lord.

He will be your shield and defense."

Michael sat bolt upright and looked around to see if anyone else could hear the voice that seemed so clear to his own ear. Everyone around Michael was fast at work either reading or writing with the notable exception of Nick Freeman who was frowning at Michael. Nick was seated clear across the room, however, so Michael had no concern that he had overheard the angel's words. After about a half hour of concentrated effort Ms. Adams announced time for lunch break and each student rose to grab coats and lunch bags from the closets at the side of the classroom.

Frank bumped into Michael and invited him to sit with him in the cafeteria. "I'd like you to get to know my friends Bobby and Raffi , so let's hang together, O.K.? They're pretty cool kids even if they do spend time with some of the girls," Frank offered in a soft voice. Despite Frank Fenelli's size his voice was always low in volume causing Ms. Adams no end of frustration in asking Frank to repeat what he had said over and over again. Michael was eager to agree to Frank's invitation. Something internal was urging him to get to know this group of friends in a deeper way.

Bobby Savin and his twin sister Jennifer were the first to land at the lunch table where they proceeded to unwrap a veritable feast of carefully wrapped packages and bags of fresh-cut vegetables, fruits, assorted mini sandwiches, chips and even a Tupperware container of onion and sour cream dip. The extra goodies, especially the dozen or so fresh baked chocolate chip cookies, were meant to be shared among the group that quickly assembled there. Sylvia Murphy was particularly pleased with the extra food since their family was on a tight budget while Mr. Murphy was looking for a new job. Her usual small peanut butter and jelly sandwich never completely satisfied the willowy girl who stood a good head above the rest, including Frank.

While Michael and Frank were getting settled on the bench seats Kerry Jordan joined the group. Frank blushed at the sight of Kerry with her waist length dark hair and radiant smile. Kerry was not only growing more gorgeous by the day, she was also extremely popular and usually acknowledged as one of the brightest girls in the class. Many would say that Jennifer with her blonde good looks and huge vocabulary was her closest rival, but also her best friend. The two girls instantly put their heads together. After several whispered exchanges they began some innocent teasing of Sylvia about her recent misadventures. In trying to learn how to figure skate on the local frog pond just behind the school, Sylvia had taken some nasty spills.

"Those frogs must have come out of hibernation yesterday, Sylvia. You hit the ice about forty-two times. Those crashes caused quite a quake just under your landing gear!" Sylvia laughed good-naturedly along with them, knowing she was due for some teasing from her charming buddies. Then she pretended to pout, "You two have had skating lessons for years! Just give me a chance, will you?" Jennifer and Sylvia reached for some veggies to dip into the Tupperware bowl that sat in the center of the table.

Raffi, an olive skinned boy several inches shorter than the rest spoke up in Sylvia's defense. With his warm brown eyes and easy smile he settled into the fray with a quick quip, "Sylvia has great balance from years of ballet. I ought to know cause I've had to attend all her recitals!" He poked Sylvia in the ribs causing her to giggle. "She'll be cutting figure eights all around you two in under a week. I'll bet a meatball sub on it," he grinned good-naturedly. Raffi had arrived straight from the food counter to claim his seat next to his pal, Sylvia. They had been next-door neighbors and buddies since kindergarten. He particularly appreciated Sylvia's lack of squeamishness about catching reptiles and insects for his terrarium. They often studied their glass-encased captives together then set them free a week or two later if they felt that their subjects were languishing in any way. Both were very soft hearted toward animals and talked about future careers as vets.

Michael settled easily into this group of friends and found himself laughing and joking with them throughout lunch. When the cafeteria doors finally opened to the outside everyone quickly cleared their food and paper goods, recycled their drink cans and bottles as they had been instructed since pre-school and headed for the playground. The efficiency of the clean-up and quick migration outside didn't especially reflect a cooperative attitude as much as the desire of the fourth, fifth and sixth graders to get a much needed change of scenery. The opportunity to let loose pent up energy inspired the sixth graders as they immediately set up an impromptu game of soccer. Although Frank was a fifth grader he was sought out for one of the sixth grade teams because of his strength as a runner. He asked Michael to join him, but Michael refused. Gym had worn out the little reserve of energy Michael had. Besides, Michael wanted to stick with his newfound friends and get to know them better. With the sun already casting long shadows on the snow, Michael found himself heading into new territory in the schoolyard, with five smiling kids who would mean more to him than he could imagine at this moment in time.

CHAPTER 4

As the group trudged off toward the edge of the playground that sloped toward the frog pond each individual quieted down and grew thoughtful. Bobby opened up a topic of conversation, which had remained unspoken among the friends at lunch. "I think I'm in trouble this afternoon because I couldn't do last night's homework."

"You didn't even try it?" questioned Sylvia with a look of concern.

"I couldn't stomach making Chad Charmer into a hero. He's a bitter little wizard on a power trip if you ask me," Bobby replied.

"Well, you'll get a zero for that homework assignment for sure," added Kerry, "but I know what you mean. It was really hard for me to write on that topic, too. I couldn't do the bonus question. I felt like I was participating in something wrong if I created a witch's spell."

Michael was glad that the others were expressing problems with the story and homework project. He spoke up, "I kept trying to write a good report on Chad and it was the most difficult assignment yet this year. I thought that it was my flu bug or whatever that kept me focusing, but now I see that it's more than that."

"Kerry, I struggled with writing the spell, too! Turns out, I gave into my fear of facing Ms. Adams without the finished homework!" Jennifer was leaning against the chain link fence that separated the school property from the town conservation land and frog pond. She stood up straight with a look of determination on her face, "I don't want my brother to take all the heat for not having done his homework. I did mine, but I'm ripping it up. I wrote a spell and I'm ashamed that I did. It isn't what Jesus would want us to be doing, and that's for sure."

Michael heard the name of Jesus spoken reverently by Jennifer. He recognized that this group of friends was special because of their commitment to their Christian faith. Each one of the kids attended different denominational churches, came from different Christian traditions, but was connected by a deep love of Jesus and mutual respect for one another. If Michael considered himself part of this inner circle, he was the exception to the rule. Michael and his family knew Sylvia and her folks because they all worshipped together. It was a recently built church with a brand new pastor. This faith community was recently touched by the power of the Holy Spirit and was spoken of as being "on fire with revival." Michael understood this to mean that everyone loved going to church because no one knew what would happen next. There were many wonderful miracles as a result of the excited praise, worship, song and dance that spontaneously broke out during prayer and healing services. Sylvia's cousin Lauren had her hearing restored in her right ear. Everyone in town knew that Lauren had been almost totally deaf in that ear since suffering from severe ear infections that had plagued her during her toddler years. "How lucky we are to have Pastor Tommy and such a great church to attend," Michael thought.

Despite differences in their church services and some of their beliefs, the friends found more to unite them than to separate them, especially in their outspoken love of Jesus and in their Spirit led prayer. They all felt disturbed by the introduction of witchcraft to the teaching agenda of the fifth grade and hated having to read the Chad Charmer book. That much was obvious.

"Didn't you get the creeps when we had to listen to the chapter about the séance at the Dragonfly School of Wizardry?" asked Michael.

"Yeah, the darkened room that Ms. Adams insisted on added to the coldness in the pit of my stomach the minute she started reading about the calling up of spirits," agreed Sylvia.

"I sure wish we could stop listening to all of this stuff. It puts down Christians as a bunch of idiots and makes out that the only ones that are cool and have power are the witches and wizards," noted Bobby.

"That couldn't be further from the truth, you guys! And we all know it but are afraid to speak up for ourselves!" Kerry fairly yelled this at her friends.

To everyone's surprise, it was Michael who spoke up in a clear, strong voice. Michael began repeating the words he heard Benedict whisper in his ear. "I take authority over you spirits of witchcraft in the name of Jesus of Nazareth. I cast you to the feet of our Savior so that he can dispose of you as He wishes. I release the power and truth of the Word of God in this school. I pray for the gift of knowing the truth from the lies told to us in this place."

The other friends nodded their heads in agreement and pronounced a solemn "Amen." Raffi grinned from ear to ear, "That was awesome, Michael! Who taught you to pray like that?"

Michael replied softly, "It was just something I overheard," and as he looked up he caught a wavering glimpse of Benedict who appeared to be extremely amused.

Sylvia, with sparkling brown eyes winking at Michael added, "Lord, help us to tell our teacher that we don't want to listen to that book about witches and wizards during Literature. Know what? I'm ripping up my assignment the minute we get into class!"

The recess bell rang and the kids in the schoolyard dispersed to line up according to various homerooms. The friends that had been in prayer together fell into a fifth grade line headed for Ms. Adams class. Huge ten foot tall angels marched along at each warrior's side, swords flashing and armor clanking in a dimension unheard and unseen by anyone on the playground, except Michael who had eyes to take it all in.

The six newly bonded spiritual warriors gathered together outside their classroom door. While others were rummaging around in lockers or heading for the restrooms they stood quietly locked into what appeared to be intense but quiet conversation. The angels surrounding them grew radiant as the group exchanged words. In turn each one spoke. Prodded by Benedict's counsel Michael was first, "Do you kids know how to pray on the whole armor of God?

It's from the Book of Ephesians in the Bible and it protects you when you go into battle for God."

"Know it? We've been doing it for months here just before school starts each morning, because we've been taught to do it at the Bible camp meetings. Mr. Christopher taught us how to pray on protection," Bobby spoke up.

Raffi added, "I happened to learn it at C.C.D. last year. My teacher loved this prayer so much; we opened with a different version of it every time we met. If you don't mind, I'll start us and everyone can pitch in.

"Father, we place on our heads the helmet of salvation. We know who we are in Jesus. We belong to Him. We ask you to help us think His thoughts and to call to mind His words," Raffi spoke with authority and as he did so golden helmets appeared on each of them.

"Human minds are the great battlefield. The enemy's spies are always spreading lies, trying to confuse Christians and deceive them!" Michael heard this voice as clearly as that of his friends, but he knew it came from his great guardian, Benedict. Michael thought of all the confusion surrounding the Chad Charmer book. He knew and understood that witchcraft was wrong, but somehow the story being read had seemed so wonderful, so intriguing to him just a few days ago. Michael gazed back at the kids he considered his new friends. He was amazed at their prayer and their wisdom.

Jennifer, slight and spunky, broke into a sprightly grin. She spoke up next, although she began slowly needing to remember what part of the whole armor of God got prayed on next, her words were serious and had immediate effect.

"We put on the breast plate of righteousness, Lord. This will guard our hearts. We love you best of all. Our hearts belong to you, Jesus. We will love one another as you love us, too!" No sooner had Jennifer finished than burnished pieces of golden armor covered each of them from neck to waist. The chain mail connecting the pieces was supple as they moved and didn't restrict them at all.

Bobby, Jennifer's twin brother, stood beside her and was the next to pray on a piece of the armor. "The belt of truth is next. We put it on so we will know truth from a lie. Lord, give us a lie detector so we can be alert at all times." The belt appeared with letters etched into it. "**THE WORD OF GOD**," it read. Buckled into the belt was an amazing, bright and shining sword. Each young warrior immediately had an impressive weapon at his or her command. Some were brighter, sharper and longer than others.

Bobby continued praying, " Let's remember to speak the truth always. Jesus is the TRUTH."

"Amen!" The group replied.

Sylvia was impatiently waiting her turn to speak, "Jesus, let us put on the shoes of the Gospel of peace. We need to walk in your peace, not in confusion or doubt or fear. The enemy wants us to be afraid to speak up for what we believe." Sylvia paused in her prayer and added in a half joking manner, "Let's put on our army boots and get going before we're late for class!"

She did not realize the powerful effect her words had in the spirit realm. The angels encircling the group bent low and tied a combat boot onto each prayer warrior's foot. The boots were new and tough and looked like they were rugged enough for the long journey ahead.

"Wait a minute," said Sylvia as she lifted a clenched fist in front of her. "Don't forget the shield of faith. You know we are gonna get attacked if we go to battle on this. Our faith will give us courage when those fiery darts of the enemy come flying toward us."

"Yeah, fiery darts of the enemy in the form of some nasty words from our dear Ms. Adams. Do you think any of us will end up in detention for speaking up against that book?" Kerry asked with a quiver in her voice. She was the fifth in the group to speak.

"Don't worry, if you're kept after we all stay after," Michael reassured her, "We're in this together to the end!"

Raffi piped up, "Don't forget we have the Sword with us! Maybe we can get the enemy to back off with some quotes from the Bible. Jesus made Satan back off with a few well-placed jabs of the Sword. He said "It is written!" and sent Satan back to hell where he belongs! With imaginary thrusts and jabs Raffi danced around in the hallway causing the rest of the group to laugh loudly.

"That's enough horseplay out in the hall. Get into class and get seated, NOW!" Ms. Adams voice rang out as sharp as any fire alarm.

Jennifer quickly closed the prayer, "Father send your Glory to cover our backs and to protect us. Remember what Mr. Christopher always told us? That God's joy is our strength!"

The friends found their seats in various parts of the room. Desks were grouped in fours in this classroom, but none of the prayer warriors were seated together. Ms Adams, a portly woman of about twenty-eight years of age, sat on the edge of her desk and pulled her glasses down the bridge of her nose. Ms. Adams' Irish ancestry shone in the burnished red-gold hair that was her finest feature. It was cut short so that soft curls framed her face. She brushed away a tendril from her forehead with an impatient flick of her fingers and slipped off the desk while pounding on the cover of her hardbound edition of the Charmer book.

"Let's get settled quickly so that I can continue reading from Broomsticks Arise. As you know this is the first of six books written about the young wizard Chad Charmer. When we left off, Chad was about to cast a spell against that nasty cousin of his, Winslow Worm."

Kerry's hand shot up. "Yes, Kerry, if you need a copy to help you follow along there is a dozen at the library corner. I know some of you prefer to just close your eyes and let your imaginations go wild, " Ms. Adams fairly glowed with these final words.

"Excuse me, Ms. Adams, but I object to reading, Broomsticks Arise, in class. It teaches about a religion that I'm not comfortable with and I know there are others in here who feel the same way." Kerry's face turned bright pink with the stress of making this proclamation.

Ms. Adams mouth dropped open and then her lips compressed into a hard thin line. She snapped her glasses back into place and focused her smoldering eyes on Kerry. "What exactly do you mean by asserting that this book is promoting a religion, Kerry! I think you have some nerve interrupting us like this!"

Kerry looked down for a moment while her angel drew close in a protective stance. A dark entity entered the room, tall in stature and sporting a crown bearing symbols of witchcraft, the prominent pentagram glittering with a thousand tiny crystals. The demon stood defiantly with one hand resting on the book at the edge of Ms. Adams' desk.

Michael could see this entity and began praying silently under his breath for a counter move by God. Suddenly Michael was aware of the awesome angelic being covering Kerry with powerful wings. It bent low to Kerry's ear and then whispered some words of encouragement. Kerry whispered under her breath, "Greater is HE that is in me than he that is in the world." Michael heard both exchanges and knew Kerry's prayer exactly reflected the angelic message.

Kerry's breastplate shone with an adamantine brilliance. The words Ms. Adams spoke with harshness bounced off Kerry and didn't sink into her heart. Kerry's powerful angel bent near again and whispered words of wisdom into his charge's ear. With sudden inspiration, Kerry lifted her eyes and met her teacher's gaze with a calm confidence. "That book teaches kids to depend on witchcraft for power. Chad is the hero. He's a very likable hero, an underdog, really. How does he solve all his problems? With witchcraft!"

"I don't understand your problem with this Kerry, it's just a fantasy! There are many stories and fairy tales written in the past that use witches and witchcraft as part of the plot. All of a sudden you've got a big problem with this one! Explain!" snapped Ms. Adams.

"The problem is that witchcraft is a real popular religion today and the Charmer book shows how to use it to get out of trouble. Those who don't practice this "gift' are looked down upon as ignorant "Quizzicals." The "Quizzicals," who are Christians like me, are made out to be real jerks. Ms. Adams, the old fairy stories you're talking about are probably those like Hansel and Gretel or Snow White. The witches fought against the good characters. They were on the side of evil using evil powers. No way would witches be the heroes."

Bobby raised his hand next. His belt of truth began to glow as he spoke, " You know what, Ms. Adams, if you take God out of the picture, there is no spiritual power that is good. People think white witchcraft is good. Right?" Bobby scanned the room to see many shaking their heads in agreement with this statement. " Wrong! Our Christian faith tells us it's a lie made by Satan to suck folks into thinking that we can be powerful, like God. It's the same old story. You can read about it in Genesis if you want." Bobby was amazed at the words that flowed from His mouth. That defense came out of nowhere! "Wow, it's just like what the Bible says! You don't have to prepare ahead of time, the Holy Spirit will give you the words to say," Bobby whispered to Kerry who nodded in agreement.

Ms. Adams got red in the face, "Bobby, you know that Genesis is in the Bible and the Bible is not allowed in a public school classroom." The dark entity grinned and draped his black gossamer wings around the teacher's shoulder.

Raffi raised his hand and when acknowledged agreed with Bobby's point, "If the Bible can't be read here, then Broomsticks Arise shouldn't be allowed here either. Witchcraft is like a slap in the face to God. He asks us to depend on Him, to trust Him, and to look to Him for help and answers when we're in trouble." Raffi's angel drew up to his full height, which was majestically superior to that of the dark angel.

"This is not a theology class, Raffi, so let's stop talking about what God wants and expects, okay? Explain why you think a book about witchcraft should be banned in our classroom. What do you mean about the popularity of witchcraft today? I think you three kids are loony tunes! Pardon my frankness here." Ms. Adams' felt her classroom authority threatened. She stood in a defensive pose, her arms folded across her chest and yet there was a light of curiosity in her eyes that opened the door for more discussion.

Raffi drew in a great breath and exhaled before launching into his explanation. "My pastor told us just last Sunday that right now all over the world people are hungry for spiritual experiences. They don't know God. They don't know how to pray. They're just dyin' to get answers for their problems."

"That's really true," piped in Sidney, "My mom and aunt both go to this tarot card reader because they want to find out all kinds of things about stuff like my aunt's boyfriend and whether or not he's going to pop the big question if you know what I mean!" Sidney, sitting across from Raffi, arched her eyebrows in a dramatic and comical way.

"Sidney, I think you're off track here, but let's relax a bit. I think we're all getting too uptight," Ms. Adams tone softened and she smiled seemingly amused with the notion of the fortuneteller. "I have even consulted with tarot readers and psychic hotlines from time to time. I'm sure it's all in fun. Nothing wrong with a little innocent fun, is there?"

The dark entity grinned from ear to ear-revealing sharp glittering teeth. His smile looked to Michael like a snake baring its fangs before a strike. Michael shivered and felt coldness in the pit of his stomach. "Don't be afraid of what you are seeing. It cannot harm you. I am showing you this for a purpose that you will soon understand." Benedict rested a hand on Michael's shoulder and Michael felt instantly comforted.

Michael saw that Sylvia was next to raise her hand and she waved it like a flag of protest, "Sorry, Ms. Adams, but that's exactly what Raffi was talking about: people lookin' for answers in all the wrong places! Only God's got the right answers."

"I thought I made myself quite clear, here, young lady that this was not going to turn into a discussion about God. I have the perfect right to consult whomever I please about my personal future!" Ms. Adams drew herself to her full height and glared at Sylvia in a most intimidating way.

Jennifer turned her head toward her twin brother at the group seating directly behind her. Jennifer's expressive eyes flashed disapproval and she whispered to Bobby, "You bet she can consult with anybody she pleases. She's got a hot line going right to hell with those tarot card readers and psychics telling her half truths and outright lies."

"Jennifer, I see you have some comments to make. Would you care to express them to the whole class?" Ms. Adams was getting deeply annoyed at this point. She was beginning to snap her fingers at people and that was a sure sign of trouble that the whole class could clearly read.

Jennifer attempted her most innocent look and replied, "I was simply agreeing with you Ms. Adams, that you have a right to consult whoever you want to!" Michael's angel looked momentarily taken aback by this unexpected comment from one he could clearly see had a guardian from God standing firmly beside her. Jennifer continued after seeing the calming effects of her comment on Ms. Adams, " It's the same thing with all those who choose to practice witchcraft and all the other way-popular New Age practices that go along with it. Everyone has the right to their own religion and the right to their opinions. On the other hand, I shouldn't be forced to participate in another person's religion by having to write spells and such. There is a big power play going on here, you know. "

Touched by her angel's hand, Jennifer looked quite firm and spoke with an authority and intelligence that was beyond her years. "You can see kids high on the occult all around us in school if you are tuned into it, Ms. Adams. Look at those who wear pentagrams, you know, the five-pointed star within a circle. They're all thinking they get power from it. Look at those who wear crystals for healing and protection. They are all about pagan religion worshipping Gaia. They think that's "Mother Earth" or the goddess of nature or some other idol. That's their right. I choose the cross of Christ to depend on! I believe Jesus is the only real power and His protection lasts forever." Jennifer closed her speech, lowering her eyes and instinctively fingering the small gold cross glittering on a thin chain around her neck. Jennifer was the best debater of the group, but she surprised even herself with what she had said to Ms. Adams. Behind her hand she whispered a comment to this effect to her brother, which Michael could overhear.

Jennifer's friends held onto their crosses and several others began doing the same. Some were whispering prayers under their breath sensing the battle that had been engaged. Sitting in shadows that indicated areas of the room where the dark side of the warfare was launching attacks, six kids grabbed onto either crystals or pentagrams and began caressing them lovingly.

Nick dressed all in black and sporting a pentagram began whispering something under his breath. Angels and demons became visible to Michael throughout the room and they began heated swordplay with one another. Just when a demon appeared to get the upper hand Sylvia whispered a prayer and the evil angel shrank and exploded like a dark, oily bubble. Meanwhile the verbal battle continued in class.

"You're right, Jennifer, my whole family practices white witchcraft and I'm proud of it!" Fawn, better known as 'Moonbeam,' spoke right out. In our creed we promise that we will harm no one. What goes around comes around. Our craft comes from ancient practices that go back to the Druids and to other ancient cults. We draw on the powers of nature. We cast spells to change events for our own good. I guess you might even call our spells a kind of prayer wish."

"Your own good might be like my worst nightmare!" Jennifer retorted immediately.

"Who cares if it is, Jenny? I for one don't!" boomed Nick who felt he had been quiet long enough. "I made no such promise about not casting no spells, so you'd better watch your back!" A small demon perched on Nick's shoulder snickered with delight. Jennifer sat scratching her head trying to count the negatives to decipher the exact meaning of Nick's words. She got the general picture that he meant what he said as a threat. Ms. Adams dismissed Nick's nasti-ness with a toss of her head and a barely audible, "Hush, now, Nick. Let's not get personal here."

Bobby clenched his fist on his desk and invisibly took hold of the sword of the Spirit. "In the Bible, the Lord says that **every** prac-tice of witchcraft is, " detestable" in His sight. That means it makes Jesus sick to his stomach when he sees it! It kind of makes me want to puke too!" Bobby glared at Nick as he made this final comment.

"This conversation is getting way out of hand and your being gross, Bobby. Unless you and your friends want double your math homework I suggest that you settle down now! Let's just continue with the book, shall we?" Ms. Adams looked tired and disgusted with the turn of events in the room, but the rest of the class looked completely engaged by what was being said. Some kids looked angry and confused, others were thoughtfully considering the comments offered so far and were nodding agreement with the friends from time to time.

"I really think that book is the whole point of this discussion, Ms. Adams, and we are saying that if the Bible is not allowed in a public school classroom, then a book like Chad Charmer shouldn't be allowed either! " Bobby spoke this out without even raising his hand. It was a bold move bringing the whole issue right around again to the choice of reading material gripped firmly in Ms. Adam's hand.

"Look, all of you, I'm tired of this discussion and we don't seem to be getting anywhere with it. Besides, our allotted time for reading Chad Charmer has elapsed. I am curious to know how many of you object to my reading this book. Please raise your hands right now!" she demanded in a sharp voice.

Immediately six hands shot up, and after the briefest moment of hesitation, two more kids raised their hands, also. Michael turned around and smiled at his friend Frank and Maria Gracia who had just joined their church last week along with her parents and two younger brothers. Encouraged by Michael's appreciative smile, Marie and Frank raised their hands higher.

"I count eight of you. That's exactly one-third of this class. I think what I need to do is make an appointment with our principal, Mr. Gladstone, during your library class tomorrow. Those who feel strongly about this issue will be asked to join me in his office. This discussion will continue with him! We'll see how all of this turns out tomorrow." Ms. Adams was clearly bringing closure to the discussion for the time being.

In every corner of the room angels and demons alike lowered their swords, but the determined looks in both ranks and the occasional brandishing of an angelic sword was proof that the battle would continue.

"Now get out your math books so we can get some work done!" Ms. Adams turned to the chalkboard and began to write several pages numbers down.

Michael could see the dark demon resting his heels on Ms. Adams' desk, cool and confidant. Michael continued to pray under his breath. Benedict sauntered over and jabbed the evil lord with the tip of his sword. "You've had your way here long enough! Get out!" The mighty angel's words caused the demon to jerk out of Ms. Adam's chair, his hoofed feet landing on the floor with a thud. "The shed blood of Jesus is against you! I demand that you leave now!" Benedict commanded in a tough curt tone. Michael watched in amazement as the evil entity cowered and crawled out of the room. His opinion of Benedict as his guardian soared.

"You've won today, but I'll be back," the enemy spat as he slunk out the door.

Michael congratulated Benedict under his breath. "You're awesome!" He said with heartfelt praise. "I couldn't have done it without your prayer support, Michael!" Benedict grinned. "Now, pay attention to Ms. Adams or you'll not be able to do that math homework she's about to assign!"

CHAPTER 5

The rest of the day flew by and finally concluded with Ms. Adams scolding Jennifer and Bobby about the missing essay on Chad as a Hero. Sylvia's lack of homework went unnoticed because she had handed in an extra credit essay on "My Favorite Fantasy Story." Sylvia wasn't about to draw attention to the fact that she had tossed her comments on Chad into the "round file," as her teacher liked to call the wastebasket. Ms. Adams seemed to take delight in giving the twins an additional writing assignment having to do with the importance of being responsible about homework. "It's not as if we have ever been irresponsible about our homework until today," Jennifer whispered to her brother and to Sylvia who was within earshot. Her voice had an edge to it, as if she was holding back a few unshed tears. Sylvia smiled sympathetically and not without feeling a twinge of guilt.

"Wait until Dad hears about this, he'll probably be on my case tonight!" confided Bobby to Michael. "Pray for me that I don't get grounded," Bobby sighed with a grimace. Ms. Adams left the room with the box of mini donuts under her ample arm. She was disgruntled and clearly not in a sharing mood.

"Thanks a lot for putting Ms. A in a terrific mood, you mush brains," yelled Nick to the group as they left the room together.

"I hope you don't plan anymore wonderful afternoon discussions like this one," countered Moonbeam who was wearing a disdainful expression on her face. She pulled a strand of black hair from in front of her eyes and tucked it daintily into a bun in the back of her head. She loved to drag her long black fingernails across the pallor of her forehead for dramatic effect. Her nails reminded Michael of the talons on the owl ornament on Ms. Adams' desk. He turned to look at it as he passed through the classroom doors. The malevolent glassy eyes glowed eerily in the owl's face. "Yes, this will be quite a battle," Michael thought.

The group, now numbering six, split up once they reached Main Street, with Bobby, Jennifer, Kerry and Sylvia heading north further into the shopping district and Michael and Raffi turning south toward the residential end of town.

"Bobby has a sweet tooth," remarked Raffi, "and he talked the girls into stopping at Frosty's for a sundae. Do you want to join them or should we head home?"

"Let's head home, Raffi. There's something I want to talk to you about, something that I have been seeing and hearing, Raffi, well...you probably are going to think I'm crazy if I tell you!" Michael tucked his chin deep into his jacket and looked at the icy sidewalk in front of him instead of looking at his friend's expression. Raffi on his part had a quirky smile playing on his lips and leaned his shoulder into Michael, "What's up? After today, I'm ready to hear some good news, some interesting news."

"Well, this is definitely good news because I believe this is a gift from God and it's more than interesting; It's amazing! I think it can help us win this war against the reading of the Charmer book in class. Last night I had a dream. It was more like a vision. You know, like in the book of Joel in the Bible where it says that God would pour out His Spirit in the last days. That old men would dream dreams and that young men would see visions?"

"Yeah, I remember that passage, Father Bill preached and taught on it not that long ago. You know, this is kind of weird but Sylvia mentioned that Pastor Tommy talked and taught about that Bible passage last week at the youth group Bible study at her church," responded Raffi with eagerness.

"Well, I think that the time that Joel spoke about is right here and right now, because that is just what is happening to me,"

Michael looked up and gave Raffi a hard look to see if he was being heard and understood.

"Explain, I want the rest of the story!" Raffi's wide-eyed expression and eager tone was a green light for Michael to pour out the details of his dream vision, and the ability he had been given to see into the realm of the spirit. When he got to the end of the story, complete with details of the initial clash in the classroom between God's angels and the dark angels, Raffi exhaled a long and deep sigh. It was almost as if he had been holding his breath through the whole story.

"I almost forgot to tell you that charming owl ornament on Ms. Adams desk has a dark spirit attached to it. It's all part of the battle plan as I see it. I think it's there to get us sucked into the occult, " Michael concluded. There were a few minutes of silence between the two boys and Michael grew a little uneasy, half fearful that Raffi would reject Michael's visions as ridiculous imaginings.

"Wow, this is awesome, Michael," Raffi responded with a grin growing on his face. "You can keep all of us posted on what you are seeing and what the enemy's moves are, can't you?" Michael heaved a big sigh of relief, "I was afraid you wouldn't believe me!"

"No way, I could sense and feel that battle going on and I know what you are saying is true. I even felt my skin crawl and a cold feeling in the pit of my stomach when I passed Ms. A's desk. I might not be able to see those enemy agents, but I certainly can sense them! You are right on, Michael my man! Wait until I tell the others this news. You don't mind if I tell them, do you Michael?" Raffi's response was genuine and supportive.

After the briefest hesitation Michael answered, "No, I'd be happy if you told them, Raffi. They're more apt to believe this coming from you than me anyway. They know you better and they trust you."

"Don't worry, leave it to me!" Raffi called as he swung into the lane leading to his home.

Michael opened the door to his small white ranch house and smelled brownies baking in the oven. It was a wonderful welcoming scent and he suddenly felt overwhelmed by the day's events. He wanted to share the secret of his ability to see visions with his mom, but was timid to do so. "Would she think I've gone bonkers on her?" Michael mused. He felt tired and wished he could just pile into the comforters on his bed and sleep, but instead he headed for the kitchen and got an affectionate hug from his mom. Her hair was frosted with flour and the sight made Michael laugh for the first time in many hours.

"Tell me everything about your day, spare no detail," Mom turned and opened the oven door slightly to see how the brownies were progressing.

"You're home early," Michael countered, "How come?"

"I got all the briefs typed for Mack, so he told me to head home around two today, in consideration for the several late nights I spent helping him to prepare for the O'Connor case." Michael's mom worked in a local attorney's office. She was kind of a one-woman legal secretary and office manager for the kindly Mack McDougal. Mack was the antithesis of every lawyer joke ever bantered around. He was charitable almost to the point of bankrupting himself with pro bono work. "That means Mack takes on all kinds of charity cases, and cases he just plain believes in because that's just the kind of man he is," Mom had explained to Michael months before when she had taken the job. Michael smiled up at his mom and realized for the first time that some of the white in her hair was for real, not just frosting from the flour.

"Mom, I've had a tough day and I want to talk seriously to you and Dad about what's been going on, but first can I just sit and have a snack and veg out? I need some rest, I think, before I start explaining about everything that's been happening in Ms. Adam's class."

"Sounds serious, Michael. I hope nothing is wrong with you. Are you in trouble in class?" Mom asked with a hint of worry in her voice. Michael shook his head to say no, but wasn't sure that was exactly accurate.

"Well, Dad will be home early today too. He's driving up from Chicago and started out at noon. He's been on a sales call today," the wavering note of anxiety remained in Meghan's voice. With that pronouncement both Michael and his Mom could hear the rattling wheeze of Dad's ancient yellow Chevy Impala as it shuttered to a stop in their driveway. Bill Minotti hopped out of his "banana," and with his briefcase slung over his back like a school bag ran up the terraced stone steps to the front entrance.

The two people he loved best in this world greeted him at the door. Each looked like they were bearing the weight of that same world on their shoulders. Bill commented on the tray of thick brownies that were cooling on the kitchen counter and then pulled his wife and son to the living room couch were they could, "spill the beans," as he put it.

"Meghan, what's wrong? You didn't burn the dinner because all I can see and smell are the brownies and they look just fine to me!"

"Tell your dad and me exactly what's going on in Ms. Adam's room, Michael, and don't hide anything because we'll just find out anyway!" Mom's prodding was a little sharp and had an edge of anxiety to it. She was tired and hoped that Michael was not the bearer of bad news from school.

Michael sat stone still, glassy eyed and more than a little weary. Then he launched into a minute-by-minute retelling of the conflict over the book. "And I think Jennifer and Bobby may get into trouble at home over the missing homework assignment," Michael concluded. Benedict suddenly appeared leaning against the kitchen counter. He was silent and wore a slightly amused expression.

Michael's jaw dropped open and he immediately regretted not sharing his "special gift" with his parents. All the details of the spiritual warfare were missing from Michael's account. "I just don't want to get into all of that now and what if they don't believe me!" were the thoughts that popped into Michael's weary head. Michael mouthed the words, "Sorry, Benedict!" and was answered by a radiant smile.

"Michael, we side with you on this one," his father responded. "I'm going to talk with Mack to see if we can attack this from a legal angle," Mom spoke with professional determination, but the hug she gave Michael was warm and comforting. "But for right now, I think I'll call for a pizza and put together a nice salad to go along with it!"

Before Mom could reach for the phone it rang. Raffi's voice, slightly hoarse, was on the other end. "Hey, Michael, I just wanted you to know I spoke to the others and they are very cool with everything you told me…"

"Really? Everyone believed what I told you about the owl and the battle in the classroom?"

"Michael, make it a short phone call if you are as hungry as we are!" called mom from the kitchen.

Michael waited while Raffi hesitated and finally confided, "Well, Bobby was skeptical. He thinks your visions are a little over the top. Bobby's a 'let's wait and see' kind of guy."

Michael heaved a sigh of relief that Bobby didn't call him a total nut, "That's fine. To tell you the truth, I am too. I want to see where all of this goes and why this is happening to me!"

"Listen, I've got to go. Homework calls," Raffi closed with, "God go with you and with all of us!" and Michael hung up with an "Amen!" He immediately thought how weird that was. He'd never said good-bye on the phone to anyone before with the word, "Amen," but under the circumstances it seemed very natural.

Everything seemed prayer related to Michael now. He found himself praying over his pizza with a more fervent grace, knowing that Benedict was witnessing his every word. Pepperoni pizza arrived swiftly and Michael ate quietly but with relish. His mom and dad asked questions of Michael to see if his tone and his friend's had been respectful in the classroom. Michael answered each question as best as he could remember.

"Do you want us to get involved, tiger? I don't want that Charmer book read in your classroom. A book that teaches kids the benefits of practicing witchcraft just doesn't belong on an elementary classroom shelf, and I'm not old fashioned, just plain old God-fashioned!" Dad said, the muscles in his jaw were flexing and there was fire in his eyes as he spoke.

"Your father and I want you to know you kids don't have to fight this battle alone!" his Mother added fervently. Michael could see Benedict beaming at him as he stood near his father's right arm. "Thanks, Mom and Dad. It helps a lot to know you are there for back up and believe me I know that I am not fighting this battle alone! But for right now let's see what happens in the principal's office tomorrow. Say a prayer for us around eleven tomorrow morning!"

"You've got it!" both parents looked proud and concerned at the same time. Michael sped through his homework and felt surprised that he could concentrate at all, especially with the twenty-five math equations that he put off for last.

Bedtime was welcomed instead of resisted. The same golden light spilled onto Michael's pillow as he closed his eyes. His parents tiptoed into the darkened bedroom and were surprised by the halo of light surrounding their Michael. "He really does look like an angel," Michael's mom whispered.

Dad sat on the edge of Michael's bed while his mother hovered over his head stroking his hair lightly. Dad spoke softly and Michael opened his eyes then shut them again, too tired to focus "Let's pray, Michael. 'Father, we love you and as always we come before You in the name of Your mighty Son, Jesus. We thank you for this day and ask you to provide wisdom and protection for all of us tomorrow. Please let us walk in your will. Help us to do what is right and give Michael courage to stand up for what he knows is right; for what You want him to do!'" "Amen!" the three voices chimed together in one accord.

As Michael's parents shut the bedroom door, Benedict's shining form could be seen standing watch directly beside the headboard of the twin-sized bed. Michael smiled and lifted his hand in salute to his angelic guardian. Benedict returned the salute then fixed his gaze out the window and into the night. At first Benedict frowned then lifted his luminous eyes to the heavens. His lips, shining in the moonlight were moving in a silent prayer language that could not be intercepted by enemy agents abroad in the darkness. Benedict prayed without ceasing while Michael slept soundly.

CHAPTER 6

S hortly after dawn Michael awoke feeling refreshed. He looked around the room expecting to see Benedict, but his tall muscular form was not in evidence. Michael also woke up with the thought "This is D- day, decision day one way or the other about that book!" D-Day, as Michael called it, began with the call to prayer and the strong sense of Jesus' presence surrounding Michael.

He could smell the scent of Jesus' heavenly garden in his room and Michael's heart began to pump hard with excitement. "Lord, Jesus, I love you and I know you love me. There is nothing that is impossible to You, so I won't be afraid. I know that you are with me and that this is the battle you were preparing me for. I am ready because you are with me. Your helmet is on my head, because my mind is set on You. I know I belong to you. Your breastplate surrounds my heart. I'm gonna have a brave heart today. Help me to love Moonbeam and Nick with the kind of love you have in Your heart for them. I will wear the belt of truth and be honest and true in everything I say today and especially in the principal's office, Jesus, please give me your words. Help me speak the truth. Let me walk in the shoes of the Gospel of peace. Somehow I know that these shoes are army boots. They step on the enemy and crush him, and bring peace wherever they march. I will lift up the shield of faith," Michael lifted his left arm above his head still resting on the pillow, " There will be enemy attacks today, I just know it! But I will try not to be afraid, because my faith is in you, not in me. You will get us out of this jam! I believe in You, Jesus!"

Michael could see Benedict now and he was holding a brilliant object in a firm grip. "Arise, Michael, I have something very special to give you!" Michael jumped out of bed and landed on the cool planks of the bedroom floor.

"It's your sword, Benedict! You are willing to give it to me?" Michael could hardly believe his eyes. Benedict had turned his magnificent weapon so that the hilt was presented to Michael. The blade was huge and sharp and gleamed with a light of its own and on it was written "The Word of God." Michael was dazzled by it. "Explain what the inscription means, Benedict," Michael was more than curious to know every bit of the sword's meaning and history. "The Word...that's another name for Jesus. This sword has His name on it, Michael. It is used with the power of His name propelling it! What weapon can stand against it?" Benedict's eyes blazed.

"None!" Michael agreed heartily to this rhetorical question.

Benedict continued, "This weapon is the Sword of the Spirit of God. You will wield it against the enemy each time you quote the Word in battle, and each time you speak God's truth when tempted to tell the convenient lie. You are equipped now for battle. Carry it in your belt of truth!" Michael could see the warrior's tooled leather belt around his waist. The belt included a scabbard in which to sheath the sword. He lifted the Sword carefully and it sang like the sweet sound of a violin as he set it into his belt. It was surprisingly light and easy to handle. Michael looked at Benedict with tears in his eyes. "How can I ever thank you, my friend," Michael whispered in a voice choked with emotion.

"In a few moments you'll start getting ready for school and I'll disappear from sight, but don't think I've gone anywhere. I'm sticking really close to you. I'm near even if you can't always see me!"

"I want to see you always, Benedict. I'd really hate it now if I couldn't be with you anymore!" Michael spoke, moving toward the door of his bedroom as he followed Benedict's retreating figure.

Benedict became iridescent with all the colors of the rainbow flowing over his robes. As he spoke his form began flickering almost like that of a candle flame, "Don't worry about that now

Michael, let's just get going. We've got a lot to do today. Jesus is with us and that's the most important thing!"

"I sure know that!" Michael responded as he moved quickly toward the hallway. Benedict had vanished and all that stood before Michael was the bathroom door, where he saw himself mirrored. His reflection was not one of a warrior with a mighty weapon at his side, but one of a young man rumpled from sleep, badly in need of a facecloth and comb.

At the breakfast table Michael was unusually quiet, not wanting to mention the crisis in his classroom because it gave him a queasy feeling in his stomach. Michael also felt just a tiny twinge of guilt because he never mentioned Benedict or any of the other supernatural visions and events surrounding his life to his parents. The delight of having splendid secrets, like the gift of the Sword, outweighed the momentary feeling of wrongly concealing important information from his folks.

This was unusual for Michael who was very open and shared almost everything with his mom and dad, even the troubles he had gotten into when his mischievous nature took over. Michael reflected about how his parents sometimes had been disappointed in his behavior in the past, but had always forgiven him readily.

Forgiveness didn't mean that he got away with anything. He always had to, "clean up the mess," as his Dad would say.

There was the incident in third grade when he let all the frogs in the terrarium loose in the classroom one afternoon after science class. In the mayhem that had ensued, Mrs. Jones, his elderly teacher, had sprained an ankle jumping up on her chair. Michael had to work off his punishment big time by helping Mrs. Jones with a cleaning project which included organizing all of her incredibly cluttered closets and shelving and straightening the library area each day after school for six solid weeks.

Michael smiled as he remembered the frogs scattering in a green frenzy and the screams issuing from most of the girls as they ran for the hallway. All the girls except Sylvia, Jennifer and Kerry had lost their minds over the incident. That was the day Michael first recognized how cool Sylvia and Jennifer and Kerry really were. They had actually pitched in helping to recapture the frogs.

The poor creatures were more hysterical than any of the humans caught in the midst of Michael's prank.

Today's situation and confrontation with Ms. Adams and Principal Gladstone was far more serious than any Michael had ever faced, and he felt comforted knowing he had the likes of Jennifer, Sylvia and Kerry as well as his other friends to support him today. He needed all the bravery he could muster and said a silent prayer as he swung out the door and down the steps that were glazed with a coating of fresh snow that had fallen overnight.

Looking back at his front door, Michael smiled again at the sight of the Christmas wreath Mom had hung late last night. There was the promise of joy in the air, the promise of Christmas, which was a mere two weeks away.

"This weekend, we should be chopping down a tree at McDougal's forest and later decorating it. I can't wait," Michael thought. "If I can only get through this wretched week then I'll have some fun with my cousins." Michael's cousins Ted and Joe always came to help with their tree on the Saturday two weeks or so before Christmas, and in turn, he always went to Aunt Diane and Uncle Herb's on Sunday to help with their tree. It was a tradition that Michael longed for as he headed down the familiar sidewalk stretch that led to his school.

There was wonderful warmth that surrounded his thoughts about the upcoming Christmas preparations. "I hope we make those popcorn and cranberry garlands again. We ate more popcorn last year than we strung, and Teddy got a stomachache and had to lie down and watch movies early in the evening because he consumed so much of it, as well as cup after cup of the hot mulled cider. His stomach looked like an over stretched balloon and gurgled louder than the drain on their antique bathtub. He really did regret being such a piglet!" Michael thought. He smiled again remembering this incident. Fondness welled up within his chest for his younger cousin, who looked and acted a lot like Michael did at kindergarten age. He wished now that he could set the whole day aside and skip right to the weekend that promised so much family fun.

Suddenly the brick front of GW loomed up in front of Michael. Never before had his school looked so cold and forbidding, never before had Michael felt dread in the pit of his stomach as he faced a new day at school. The strong warm hand of Benedict pressed firmly into the small of Michael's back propelling him forward despite his reluctance. With Benedict's touch came a surge of confidence that whatever happened in that school today, Michael was not alone. "What is that Bible statement?" Michael spoke aloud. Benedict was quick to reply and Michael fairly shouted it aloud "Oh, yeah, the battle belongs to the Lord!"

The temperature had dipped overnight and with the mercury of the school's outdoor thermometer registering just under twenty degrees, there was no assembly outdoors. Everyone had entered the building upon arrival, and this procedure would likely last until the last blast of winter sometime in early March. Instead of lingering on the school steps with a few of his classmates, Michael pushed hard on the front door of the school and it opened onto the main lobby. Michael could hear his confident footsteps sound like tiny explosions as he passed by the principal's office.

There were the usual gathering of parents, kids and school personnel milling around the main office, but Michael could also see the mustering of angelic warriors and dark clad enemy agents standing at the threshold of Principal Gladstone's inner sanctum. Oh yes, today would be a day marked with warfare, that was certain, but Michael felt confident that in the end, Jesus and "his team," would win.

As he turned the corner and started down the corridor that led to his classroom, Bobby and Raffi joined Michael. "Hey, Michael, you start the day right today?" Raffi asked.

"You mean do I have on my armor? You bet I do! I hope you guys are both ready, too!" Michael responded brightly.

"Don't leave home without it, man!" shot back Bobby. The guys could see Kerry, Sylvia and Jennifer already in the classroom huddled together talking quietly. Michael took note of the angelic warriors surrounding them and glowing brightly. One was in a kneeling position strapping on Sylvia's combat boots. "Let's leave the girls alone, they obviously are late in getting prepared," Michael whispered. "I can see the angels with them and they are getting into heavenly armor as we speak," Michael said in a matter of fact tone. Bobby shot

Michael a curious look while Raffi's eyes shone with respect.

"How do you know they're not going over last night's homework?" Bobby's question contained a bit of doubt and it was clear that he was hesitant to believe everything Raffi had told him about Michael's "gift."

"Believe me, I know," Michael responded.

"I'd like to believe you," Bobby answered softly, "I just don't know." Raffi clapped Michael on the shoulder, swung his book bag onto his back and headed for his seat in Ms. Adam's room.

Sylvia passed by Raffi in the doorframe, approached Bobby and grinned, "Sorry, we were busy praying on the whole armor of God. We weren't ignoring you guys. How are you? Did you get into trouble with your folks last night? I forgot to ask Jennifer. Sylvia hesitated before continuing because a look of surprise briefly passed over Bobby's face.

"Lucky guess!" Bobby responded, thinking again of Michael's insight into what the girls were doing.

"Well, I wouldn't call my guessing you'd get into trouble with your parents exactly lucky. I'd call it a logical conclusion!"

Bobby's face turned red, "It could have been worse. The folks were mad at first, but when Jennifer explained that it was all about that stupid book, they calmed way down. As a matter of fact, Mom said that she and dad would be praying for us kids today. I have a feeling that she would have liked to have gotten more involved, but I think she and dad wanted us to get some experience 'fighting our own battles,' as dad likes to call it."

Sylvia nodded in agreement. "I've heard my folks say stuff like that too!"

Michael, leaning against the lockers, was watching a dark spirit following after Nick Freeman. Nick's gaze was fixed on the ceiling just above Sylvia and Bobby. His eyes became glassy as he began muttering under his breath. Michael's attention was drawn from Nick's face to the demon. He could see the enemy spirit, cloaked in a black velvet cape, charge toward a loose ceiling tile and began to swing from it. Michael took swift action and pushed Sylvia out of the way. "Watch Out!" he yelled as he shoved hard at a somewhat resistant Bobby.

Momentary anger flashed in Bobby's eyes. He reflexively started to push Michael back, but the crash of the ceiling tile shattering on the floor at their feet sent a shock wave of alarm through both boys and caused them to jump back even further. Bobby's expression changed to one of gratitude. "Thanks, man! How did you ever notice that tile coming loose?" he questioned as soon as the shock wore off.

"You wouldn't believe it if I told you," Michael responded with cool tone.

"Do you mean that had something to do with the devils that you see?" Bobby's reluctance to believe in Michael's gift was lifting in the light of the near accident.

"Watch out for Nick, Bobby, he's not on our side, but there's more to it than that. I believe he practices black witchcraft. He was using his evil power to cause that tile to fall. He's not like Fawn...er...Moonbeam. She's been deluded into thinking her brand of witchcraft is good. Nick is different. He knows he's into the darkness, and he's enjoying it. He doesn't have a clue that the evil one will hurt him, too, in the end," Michael explained.

Nick snapped out of his trance and shot a look of pure hatred at Michael. It was as if he knew that Michael saw exactly what he was up to, and knew that the evasive action had been taken, not by chance, but because of a revelation Michael had been given. Michael returned Nick's hateful look with one that was both sad and thoughtful.

Benedict's voice spoke softly in Michael's ear, "Pray for him, Michael, for he is one of the captives. Pray that the Lord will be merciful and free him this day."

"Why, Benedict? Why did he want to hurt Sylvia and Bobby? What have they ever done to him?"

"Evil spirits, like the one trying to control Nick, don't need a reason to want to destroy, hurt, or even kill innocent victims. The last victim is always the one who thinks they are in control of the dark power, the tragic ones who allow them to gain entrance. Feel sorry for Nick, and pray for him, Michael. Pray for him even when you least feel like doing so," Benedict's voice faded and Michael's attention shifted to Bobby who stood looking quizzically at Michael.

Bobby clapped Michael on the back saying "O.K., I do believe that something supernatural is going on here with you. Keep up the good work, Michael, and for heaven's sake tell me if you see any other attacks coming our way!"

"Thank you, Michael, I won't forget how you saved me." Sylvia was the last one to respond and she squeezed Michael's arm appreciatively.

An elderly man dressed completely in blue denim came clattering down the hall with a barrel and broom in tow. "Be careful, you kids, step away from that shattered tile. It's a wonder that one of you wasn't knocked out when that thing fell. You're just lucky, I guess," David Charlie, the school custodian, spoke rapidly punctuating what he said with quick jabs from his broom.

"You ain't seen nothin' yet!" growled Nick to no one in particular, but God's team in the hall heard the message. If Bobby needed confirmation of Nick's involvement in the falling tile incident, he certainly heard it in the menacing message and tone of Nick's voice.

Nick, accompanied by the ugly little demon, sidled up to Michael and stuck a finger in his face, "You're gonna find out that the world is against you, Michael 'ol buddy. 'Most everybody loves Chad Charmer, and you and your friends are weird, just wanting to ruin things for everybody else. A spoil sport is what they used to call guys like you." Michael felt words rising up from his throat, " Greater is HE that is in me, than he that is in the world! He is greater than all of us and His will WILL be done. Every knee shall bend to Him, Nick, even yours, willingly or unwillingly. It'll happen! If the Lord decides that book is outta here, it's outta here!"

Michael was amazed that when he spoke these words, especially the quote from the Bible, he could see the Sword of the Spirit flashing in the air. It rent a tear right in the seam that held the demon's cloak on his scaly body. Suddenly naked, the demon disappeared from sight. Nick, as if deflated by Michael's comments, opened his mouth but nothing came out. He turned on his heels and slammed into his desk, letting the full weight of his books crash onto the desktop with an angry curse.

Ignoring the foul outburst from Nick, Ms. Adams turned to the hallway to remind the "laggards," as she called them, to get themselves into the room and ready to pay good attention to her morning announcements and pronouncements. Everyone settled to his or her desks within moments of the warning bell. The first issue of the day was to check on homework, with special note being taken of Jennifer and Bobby's assignment on responsibility. They stood together and walked up to Ms. Adam's desk to hand in their separate assignments. Ms. Adams scanned them quickly to assess if they were written neatly and were of appropriate length.

Her face turned bright pink when she read a small neat message at the bottom of Jennifer's final sheet. It said, "Although we are 100% behind your demand that our children be responsible about their homework, we want you to know that we are proud of their stand against the Chad Charmer books and will support them totally in their fight to have this series of pro-witchcraft books removed from their classroom. Sincerely, Mr. and Mrs. Douglas Savin."

Jennifer cast an innocent glance toward Ms. Adams who was tapping her foot and clearly looking annoyed. Indeed, Jennifer was unaware of the note attached to the bottom of her essay. She was in the habit of asking her parents to proof read any written work, and when she got the approval for this particular assignment, she never looked it over again, but set it neatly into her English folder along with pages of notes on fantasy and fables.

"Oh, great, I see Ms. Adams is already in a super mood," Moonbeam remarked to no one in particular, but everyone in general within earshot.

"Don't worry, Jennifer, I'm sure you did a great job on your essay," Maria Gracia whispered in support of her new friend.

"Let's get on with our morning, so get out your math books, " snapped Ms. Adams, but her command was interrupted by an announcement over the loud speaker.

"Let's stand for a moment and think positive thoughts about Mother Earth and our environment. There will be a minute of silence for those who wish to pray or meditate or whatever." The disembodied voice was one of their fellow students selected to make morning and afternoon announcements at the beginning and closing of the day. No mention was made about skipping the pledge to the flag. A few chairs scraped against the flooring as a handful of student including Michael and his friends rose from their seats.

As Michael's group of friends bowed their heads reverently in prayer, Moonbeam interrupted with dramatic flair. Jumping to her feet and twirling around she pronounced, "I'd like to meditate and levitate right outta here!" This caused a few furtive giggles from the girls seated around her and a mildly amused look from Ms. Adams. Like most teachers at GW, Ms. Adams didn't enforce the rule of standing for the Pledge of Allegiance and moment of silence. It apparently was of no importance to her whether her students participated or not, as long as they were quiet and ready for her to take control of the day's activities right afterwards.

After the so-called morning exercises Raffi's hand was in the air. "What is it Raffi?" Ms. Adams annoyed look and tone returned immediately.

"He probably wants to lead us in prayer," Nick ventured with a mocking tone. Michael could see that the demon was back, perched on Nick's shoulder, but looking rumpled and a lot worse for the wear from the morning's earlier encounter.

"No, Ms. Adams, I just want to suggest that the pledge not be skipped over or replaced by other stuff. I think it's important to keep a patriotic spirit here," Raffi asserted.

"Yeah, I know you just want everyone to say that our nation is 'under God,' Nick sneered.

"That's enough, boys, "Ms. Adams interjected, "that's one more issue you can take up with Mr. Gladstone later this morning, Raffi!" Her tone let everyone know she didn't want further discussion on the matter.

CHAPTER 7

The rest of the morning shot by quickly for almost everyone in the class, except Michael, who was beginning to experience mounting dread as the classroom clock zeroed in on the hour of destiny, the eleven-o'clock library class designated for a meeting with Principal Gladstone. It didn't help Michael's confidence to focus on the malevolent eyes of the owl ornament. They seemed to follow him wherever he went in the classroom. Michael knew that this was not just his imagination, but also an attempt by the enemy to intimidate him.

"Remember, greater is HE, Michael!" Benedict reminded him more than once, and when he felt Benedict's strong grip on his shoulder, Michael felt his faith rise up within him, and he just knew that everything would turn out right.

During the last half hour before the meeting, Michael found himself working on an independent research project about wildlife on the Arctic tundra. Normally, this would have kept him focused, but not today. When he would look up from the book he was trying to read, Michael would either take note of the crawling hands of the clock, or the evil glint in the owl's eyes. He kept reminding himself that he was not alone, that his friends, both human and angelic, would be taking a stand with him. Benedict would be there. More importantly, Michael knew that Jesus himself would be present. The Bible said Jesus had promised, "Where two or more are gathered in my name, there also will I be!"

Shortly before 11:00 a.m., Ms. Adams' intercom phone rang with two short signals that meant the main office was calling. She rose from her desk and answered in the affirmative several times.

"Class, I am being called to the principal's office in advance of our meeting. Frank, you are the class monitor this week, so please be sure everyone stays on task working on their polar reports, and let me know if anyone gets out of line in here." Frank blushed at Ms. Adams' remarks. Last thing in the world Frank wanted was the job of monitor, but everyone had to take a turn at it.

The minute Ms. Adams last footfall could be heard clattering down the hallway Nick jerked back his chair and rose to his feet making as much noise as possible. "Y'all listen to what I have to say, now. I want full attendance on this book meeting in Gladstone's office. No one sits this one out, 'ya hear! Our rights to our free pick of literature is on the line here...first amendment rights, guys. No book banning little punks are gonna tell us what to read, what to do! Are you with me?" Several answered back loudly in the affirmative, others gave weak or halfhearted cheers that Nick took as backing for his cause.

Michael could see angelic and demonic activity stirring up within the room. Benedict was visible and shining brightly beside Michael's desk as were many other guardians, some with swords drawn and flashing. Next to Nick stood a demon that looked very cunning, his long hair was slicked back with some kind of oil, then braided. In his well-muscled hands he sported a curved brass scimitar that reminded Michael of the Tales of the Arabian Nights.

The dark horned spirit in the white cloak rose from the owl ornament and floated to the door of the classroom, preparing to lead the attack in Mr. Gladstone's office. It wore the purple and gold-spangled wizard's cap on its head at an angle, slightly askew. Benedict swiped at it with his sword and knocked it onto the floor. A roar of approval rose form the angelic forces. They were sticking close to their human charges, but made their strength known by flourishing of swords and arching of wide white wings. The white robed demon glared at Benedict and uttered a tangled phrase that caused the cap to levitate and land back on its horned forehead, more than slightly askew.

"Everyone settle down," demanded the unexpected voice of Ms. Adams. She began talking loudly and rapidly before even entering the classroom door. "Mr. Gladstone has decided to come down here to see us rather than having such a large group troop to the main office and try to squeeze into his conference room. It will be much more orderly that way!" Ms. Adams eyes suddenly bulged out a little and her voice turned sharp, "Now I want you to know that I will not tolerate anyone talking out of turn, or being rude to our principal, do I make myself perfectly clear?" She glared menacingly at each of God's warriors as she spoke these words, "I will deal harshly with those who step out of line!"

Before Michael's eyes, as if on cue, the large dark devil of witchcraft lunged into the room scattering a number of smaller demons that had gathered at the doorframe. They bowed and groveled at the larger devil's feet, or hooves, for they more closely resembled goat's hooves than human feet.

Michael felt a chill that sliced through him to penetrate his very bones. He closed his eyes and prayed to the Lord, "You have promised never to leave me, to always be with me. Jesus, be close to me now!" It was as if warm comforting blankets surrounded Michael the instant his prayer was done. The chill quickly dissipated. Glancing up toward his right shoulder, Michael could see the poised and powerful presence of Benedict and every ounce of confidence and courage was restored. Michael heaved a sigh of relief just as tall, dignified Principal Gladstone knocked on the classroom door and entered. Michael smiled to himself at the familiar sight of the school principal. Mr. Gladstone had an uncanny resemblance to Abraham Lincoln, which he purposefully accentuated with a beard and old-fashioned gold-rimmed glasses. Before he even spoke, Mr. Gladstone had an aura of wisdom due to his craggy brow, furrowed with many cares and responsibilities.

"May I come in and join you folks this morning? I believe we have a curriculum concern to discuss!" Mr. Gladstone didn't wait for Ms. Adams to beckon him into the room, but strode in purposefully and sat on the edge of the teacher's desk precariously close to the owl ornament.

"Welcome, Mr. Gladstone, please make yourself comfortable," Ms. Adams replied a little late for Mr. Gladstone had indeed made himself comfortable and had already taken charge of the agenda. He was a man used to getting things done as well and as swiftly as possible.

"Ms. Adams tells me that there are a number of you who have concerns about the literature she has chosen for the unit study on fantasy and folk tales." The warriors and several of the friends were nodding their heads in agreement. "Now, I would like to start the discussion on a positive note. How many here are enjoying Broomsticks Arise?" A clear majority of hands shot up in the room. "My, my, that's quite a few of you. Would someone tell me what you believe is valuable about this book?" Mr. Gladstone glanced around the room as a few hands were timidly raised, then more souls braved to volunteer answers. "Fawn, would you care to speak about this book?"

"First I want to thank you for coming here, Mr. Gladstone. It's awesome that you would take time to talk to us about the Chad Charmer book. Did you know that it's so popular that Hollywood is making a movie about it?"

"Thank you Fawn, yes I was aware that the movie is going to be released right before Easter, I believe...I know that several parent associations have endorsed the series because it gets kids interested in reading. I'm quite impressed that one of our local parent associations has also contributed positive reviews of the Charmer series. I believe the reviews ran in "The Bridgeton Breezes," our local paper." The dark angel's chest puffed up with pride and he began to swagger around behind the teacher's desk, smirking and laughing right out loud. Michael wondered why no one but he could hear the bellowing laughter, which sounded more like a hyena's howl than real joy. Michael turned around and eyed Raffi to see if he perceived any of the racket, but Raffi seemed lost in thought and wasn't registering recognition of the noise.

Raffi raised his hand to be recognized. "Raffi, do you wish to add a positive comment?" Mr. Gladstone smiled approvingly.

"Yes, Mr. Gladstone, I'm positive I read the Parent Group's statement that you are referring to, er...actually my parents read it out loud at dinner one night because they are interested in the series, too." Mr. Gladstone leaned toward Raffi as if to grasp everything said. "One of the parents supporting the series was commenting about how enthusiastic a reader her third grader had become said that she didn't care if her Marcy was reading the Satanic Bible, as long as she was reading. My parents were pretty shocked by that statement. I know that they care if what I read is good for me or not!" All of God's angels began to cheer and raise banners of Victory.

The eyes of the owl ornament glowed red with anger and the spirit of witchcraft growled with rage. Raffi shrank back into his seat as if suddenly intimidated by the oppressive noise rising from the opposition.

Benedict pressed in toward Michael and spoke with authority, "Michael, use the Sword! The Bible tells us to bind the enemy to prevent him from acting or speaking. We cannot enforce this powerful weapon with our own strength, but we can do it in the name of Jesus! Ask the Father in Jesus' name to bind the enemy from speaking and do it now, for pity sakes, before they cause more confusion and intimidation!"

Michael whispered a prayer softly yet out loud, "Father, let the dark forces be bound and unable to speak or act in the name of Jesus, your Son." The silvery sword jumped into Michael's hand and sliced through the air enforcing the command. Sudden silence reigned in the room, as both sides grew quiet. The angels bowed in respect of the name above all names and the devil and demons crashed to their knees involuntarily and were unable to move or make a sound. Michael's mouth dropped open as he realized the power unleashed by speaking the name of Jesus aloud.

"Thanks, Benedict!" Michael smiled with renewed confidence.

"Just doin' my job!" Benedict beamed.

Mr. Gladstone pondered Raffi's comment for a long moment then spoke, "I can appreciate what you are saying, Raffi, but this book is not the Satanic Bible, it's a work of fiction, and frankly I don't see what all the fuss is about. Certainly you are aware of the book's great popularity. All the world seems to be singing it's praises!"

"Mr. Gladstone, it's real exciting and I love reading about Chad. He's a cool dude. I never read nothin' I don't like, and I tell 'ya I like this book. I plan on readin' this one...and the next and the one after that. It's like I'm hooked on them. I get the creeps that a group of sissy Christians are trying to ruin the fun we are havin' in class. Ain't that right, Ms. Adams?" Nick hadn't bothered to raise his hand before blurting out his opinion, yet Ms. Adams smiled and nodded her head in approval, as did every dark spirit in the room.

"Nick, I can appreciate your enthusiasm for the book. They are rather spellbinding. I read <u>Broomsticks Arise</u> myself over the Thanksgiving holiday and although I wouldn't rank it in the same category as the great classics of fantasy like <u>The Lord of the Rings</u> trilogy by Tolkein or <u>The Chronicles of Narnia</u> series by C.S. Lewis, it did become strangely addictive. I somehow feel I must also continue to read the Charmer books as they become available." Mr. Gladstone stroked his beard thoughtfully. Although they were silent, Michael could see the glee in the eyes of the enemy agents, and felt something had to be done or said to turn the tide.

Raising his hand high, Michael leaned toward the front of the room as if spurred on by an urgent inspiration. "Yes, Michael, you look eager to say something. Go ahead."

"Well, Mr. Gladstone, it's just this. If a number of us feel strongly that there is something bad, something really evil in the message of the Chad Charmer book, can't you allow us the right to read something else? Don't we have the right to feel okay about what we are reading?" Michael was putting the ball squarely in Mr. Gladstone's court hoping that his sense of fair play would cause him to agree.

"Well, yes Michael, I guess you are right about that, but some-how I feel uncomfortable allowing a group of kids to run the curriculum in this classroom!" Ms. Adams nodded vigorously in the back of the room. She was perched on the radiator with the owlish demon attached to her shoulder. Her plump legs dangled and her loafer shod feet occasionally clattered on the metal of the radia-tor's flat smooth side. Her feet were not really reaching the floor and this effect made her appear much younger than she was.

"Mr. Gladstone," Jennifer's voice could be heard above the murmuring sounds that erupted in the room among all the kids. "Couldn't *you* run the curriculum for a group of us who are interested in reading some of that fine literature you just mentioned? I mean, couldn't you give us assignments and projects on say, one of the C.S. Lewis books you liked so much? We could read one of them, like the first in the series, The Lion, The Witch and The Wardrobe and discuss it with you instead of the Chad Charmer book! Couldn't we? Jennifer gazed at her principal sweetly and every angel flashed their swords above their heads to remind the demons that they need to stay frozen and out of the fray.

"How many kids are we talking about?" Mr. Gladstone's eyes brightened at this idea. Ms. Adams stood at the back of the room in absolute shock. Eight hands rose into the air without a moment's hesitation.

"You know what, I like it! It's a compromise and I like the idea! I've wanted to get connected with teaching again. I'll lead the group myself during your literature class time. Ms. Adams that's right after your lunchtime if I remember correctly. This will work! I eat lunch at that time and if you kids would bear with my munching on a sandwich we could do it! The eight of you come to the library starting tomorrow at one!"

The sudden resolution of the problem left everyone slightly off balance. Ms. Adams was disgruntled but didn't dare reveal her true feelings to Mr. Gladstone. Instead she flashed her boss the biggest smile ever seen in her classroom and spouted, "A brilliant idea, Mr. Gladstone! You are just the best mediator in the world and aren't we lucky, class, to have such a terrific and dedicated principal who is so willing to give of his time to keep you children happy!" Ms. Adams led the class in loud and sustained applause while managing to glare at Jennifer and Michael in particular. She recognized that it was their combined suggestions that led to a break down of her absolute authority in the room.

"There will be hell to pay for this, if you pardon the expression," whispered Michael to Benedict who was radiant beside him, glowing with satisfaction. Mr. Gladstone rose and strode from the room like a man on a mission, for indeed; he did have the next meeting to attend. It was a pre-town meeting budget report to go over with Superintendent Henning and he wasn't looking forward to it nearly as much as he was tomorrow's literature class with the select eight.

Bobby and Raffi gave Michael a high-five and Frank shot him a "V" for victory sign. Jennifer burst out with a heartfelt "alleluia!" while Kerry and Sylvia giggled. Fawn turned and gave the three girls a withering look. Maria Gracia applauded softly and smiled at Michael appreciatively. Michael's heart was soaring with satisfaction and he thanked Jesus and his friend Benedict softly under his breath.

Nick scowled darkly and swung around at Michael hissing, "You think you won, but you haven't. We won! We still get to read our Chad Charmer books. You're just out of it now!"

Fawn confirmed Nick's declaration by adding, "The whole rest of the class will read on without your stupid objections and inter- ruptions." Although her angry glare was directed mainly at Jennifer, this thought sobered Michael and deflated his elation. Benedict's comforting hand was on Michael's head, but when Michael looked up he could see Benedict taking a somber survey of the room and along with other angelic guardians, noting a multitude of demons perching on desktops eagerly awaiting their opportunity to gain a foothold on the minds and imaginations of the "captive audience" that formed the rest of the class.

Michael gave this concern the briefest of attention when his thought processes were interrupted by a familiar part of daily routine. The urgent clanging of the bell for recess sounded in the hallway and desktops lifted in unison as books and papers were filed away, and sacks of food emerged. Michael's stomach growled, but somehow the excitement of the morning's battle and the small victory just won dulled his response to the hunger pangs. "Join me for lunch, Benedict?" Michael queried.

"I wouldn't miss it for the world!" Benedict replied with a hearty laugh.

CHAPTER 8

" "Time for lunch and recess break," Ms. Adams announced unenthusiastically. While the students were grabbing coats and jackets, Ms. Adams made a restroom pit stop. She looked pale and visibly weary from the stress of the morning's special meeting. Although she didn't have a big part in the discussion, she had felt her authority challenged in the room and recognized the need for diplomacy and tactfulness with her boss. She was in her third year at G.W. and would get tenure in the spring. The last thing Ms. Adams wanted was an "incident" of any kind jeopardizing her standing.

There was a ripple of snickering from the whole class as the plump form of Ms. Adams trudged along at the head of the line leading the way to the cafeteria. The reason for the shared mirth was a trailing strip of toilet paper stuck to the bottom of the teacher's shoe, making her a slightly bedraggled and comical sight as she led her class to the door of the lunchroom, then turned and shuffled off to the teacher's room with a look of disgust on her highly flushed face. No one, not even apple-polishing Fawn Wainwright dared mention the toilet paper to Ms. Adams. She was ripe for an explosion of temper, and no one wanted to be nearby when that happened.

Michael's temporary high returned in the cafeteria as other kids stopped by his table to say how much they admired his standing up to the principal and Ms. Adams. "I might not agree with your choice of literature, Michael, but I think you are a pretty cool dude," offered Brad Smith, Michael's buddy and sometimes idol. Brad was the top student in the class, possibly in the whole school and had athletic ability to boot. "Why don't you join our soccer game at recess, Michael, we could use your speed and smarts!" Brad concluded. Michael was beside himself with happiness.

Jennifer also shared in the adulation of the moment and had her share of admirers and encouragement as she nibbled delicately on an apple and dipped into the yogurt she had brought for lunch. Fawn jealously noted that Jennifer looked like a queen holding court and it made her sick to her stomach to see Jennifer carrying on so. Jennifer, in all actuality, was taking things pretty much in stride. She was pleased with their victory in getting out of reading that troubling book, but was also absorbed in rubbing her blistered foot and worrying about her chances in the skating contest at the Civic Center that very weekend.

She was not sure that her double axial was perfected enough to take into the rink, in a formal public competition in front of hundreds of interested spectators and competitive parents. Her trainer insisted that she was ready, so she tried to rest in that assurance, but was more than slightly concerned about her blistered foot, which was stinging and sore. She would take it easy during recess; maybe sit with a friend or two on the bench down near the frog pond and talk skating and ballet.

Jennifer brushed her long blonde hair off her shoulders and captured the golden mane in a soft ring of elasticized red velvet. In her pine green sweater and green and red Scottish plaid kilt she looked every inch the part of a lovely Christmas elf. She smiled in spite of her sore foot as a group of her friends; Kerry and Sylvia included, scooped her off the lunchroom bench and headed out the door into the crisp December air.

Fawn headed out the door also with a small group of her friends and admirers. Her expression was sour, though, and she looked wounded somewhere even though she was in perfect if pale health. Her eyes were deeply ringed from some sleepless nights. She was plotting revenge, and some her schemes had kept her awake into the wee hours of the night.

Nick had sat off to the side by himself during lunch. Michael was aware that the owl's demon kept company with Nick but he chose to ignore what plots might be hatching in order to relish the moment of victory with Principal Gladstone. Nick's expression changed during lunch from glum annoyance to sly satisfaction. Michael gave a passing thought as to what might be going on with Nick, but no more than that as he was propelled out the door by a group of friends and admirers to join in the fray of soccer.

The frosty air was filled with puffs of condensed breath as the boys ran to and fro with the soccer ball skittering along in front of the swiftest runners. Michael was in the thick of the action and feeling every inch the hero as he scored several points for his team. Once in the break of heated action, Michael glanced over at Jennifer and the girls and waved to them happily and they responded in kind. They seemed to be cheering on Michael's every move, at least that was how Michael felt, on top of the world, really.

Nick joined the game on the sideline of action and within minutes sprawled headlong into the frost-hardened dirt. He rose from the ground cursing and rubbing his skinned hands together to remove the grit. "I'm headin' in to see the nurse, you idiots! It's lucky I'm not worse hurt or there'd be some heads rollin' in the dirt!" He shot these last words in the general direction of Michael and Raffi who were in the vicinity of Nick's accident but were blameless as to the cause of his fall.

"Aw, you tripped over yer own big feet," called Brad, half laughing at Nick's misfortune.

Once inside the building, Nick headed to Ms. Adam's room directly. He stuck his hands and head under the running faucet to cool down then gulped a few handfuls of cold running water. "Now to ruin our dear Mr. Goody Two Shoes." Nick pronounced these words with an oddly ancient voice. His comment had just enough of a sinister edge that the sound of it made him laugh to himself.

For someone as tough as Nick was thought to be, he had some quaint expressions garnered from his grandmother. Granny Freeman had raised Nick alone since his mother's death and father's strange disappearance. She did the best she could on one salary based on her skills as a hairdresser, manicurist and part-time psychic and tarot card reader. Nick's father was not noted for responsibility, so his disappearance shortly after Nick's mother passed away in a car accident was really not strange if you thought about it very hard, which Nick was not wont to do.

The strange element of the disappearance was the suddenness of it, and the fact that Willy Freeman left everything behind except for his electric guitar and the clothes on his back. Granny Freeman never spoke about the five hundred dollars that disappeared out of her top right desk drawer along with her prodigal son. Nick was just two years old at the time and had only foggy memories of his father and mother. Sometimes he vaguely remembered the scent of roses that had clung to his mother when she had rocked him to sleep. He never remembered the kisses and prayers that she had bestowed upon him in countless numbers. He was told that his love of heavy metal music was "genetic," according to his Granny and he guessed that it was passed along from Willy to himself.

The love for all things of an occult or mysterious nature was definitely something in the Freeman bloodline, because Granny was something of a psychic and channeler as was her mother before her. Granny often encouraged Nick in his interest in the "dark side," and told him again and again that she sensed powers in him that were much stronger than her own formidable abilities to see into and predict the future.

Needless to say, the Chad Charmer books fascinated Nick. He identified strongly with Chad, this underdog hero who always came up smelling like roses, no matter what skullduggery he got involved with. "It's all for the cause!" was a banner slogan at Piglet Dorm where Chad resided.

"I'm gonna cast a spell on that know it all Michael and ruin him once and for all!" Nick smirked to himself. "I need a powerful object to use for this one...and I know I need you, you beautiful, powerful owl!" Nick sidled up to Ms. Adams desk and plucked the shimmering owl off its perch. Nick could see the red eyes glow within the owl's head and felt a shiver of delight and power run through his body. He nestled the ornament into a Kleenex lined pocket of his black leather jacket then swiped the wrought-iron perch off the desk.

"Now to plant the evidence!" Nick gloated as he tiptoed over to Michael's desk, lifted the top and slid the stand under a pile of papers and notes Michael had taken on the Arctic project. Michael was not the neatest and most organized kid in the class, and the mess in his desk aided Nick's subterfuge.

"This'll sure look like Michael took the ornament. He'll get the blame and the shame! Can't wait!" Nick laughed convulsively at the perfection of the plan. Not only did he have the owl to work his black magic, he also had the blame planted squarely on Michael.

"Let's see him try and talk his way out of this one!" Nick sneered, then headed for the nurse's office for good effect. His hand was a bit tender and bleeding slightly from the abrasions, but this sacrifice was well worth the end result. Nick felt confident of it.

"The only piece missing is a lock of Michael's hair. According to Chad, all good nasty spells need the victim's hair or some other personal item. That should be the easy part. Nick fairly whistled on the way to the nurse's office, and planted a frown on his face only as he reached the room with "Infirmary," etched on the opaque glass that was paneled into the top half of the door. With his uninjured left hand, Nick knocked crisply on the wooden frame and entered to see Miss Ames, the school nurse. He had the familiar look of the walking wounded but inside Nick was fairly bubbling with excitement because his alibi was in the making. He was in the nurse's office getting patched up and not anywhere near the scene of the crime, or at least that is what he would say if anyone dare point a finger of accusation at him before the incriminating evidence was found in Michael's possession. This was the happiest and most excited Nick could remember being in a long, long time. This was the most cunningly satisfied the owl's demon had felt in a long, long time also! And so the two beings sat waiting for the nurse's attention, one a vile being of incredible age and evil, and the other a sadly deceived boy who felt smart and strong but was in reality at the lowest point of his young life.

CHAPTER 9

Nick heard the recess bell's boisterous jangle from within the nurse's office. Kathy Ames hurried to Nick's side as he sprawled on the low couch that was jammed against the green cement wall. He recoiled at Ms. Ames touch, which was gentle as she swabbed the scraped palms of his hands with antiseptic. Nick was surprised at his own reaction to Ms. Ames. He had nothing against her, but he felt a twinge of pain in his heart when he looked at her. There was something about the nurse's long dark braided hair and the scent of roses about her that reminded Nick painfully of his mother.

"There, that wasn't so bad, Nick. You're a new man and can return to class after I wash your palms with Betadine and give you a bandage or two," Ms. Ames deep and mellow voice was soothing to listen to, that Nick had to admit. He nearly smiled when he looked into her sympathetic brown eyes, but then he saw the gold cross suspended on a glittering chain about her neck.

"I'm outta here, just give me my pass back to class, Ms. Ames," Nick grunted. The sight of the cross taunted him and caused a surge of bitterness to well up within Nick. Ms. Ames began praying for Nick softly under her breath in "tongues," a prayer language that was as old as Christianity and as fresh as the moment it was spoken. The syllables were not recognizable but sounded a bit like Cherokee Indian language. Kathy Ames' angel, who took her prayer for Nick to the throne room of God, immediately understood it. The prayer spoke of mercy and forgiveness. It was a prayer of hope on an otherwise bleak afternoon.

Meanwhile, God's young warriors lined up with renewed energy. The girls were looking forward, as a group, to going to the library during the Chad Charmer reading and discussion. They were anxious to start reading C.S. Lewis' classic, The Lion, The Witch and The Wardrobe.

Kerry commented to Sylvia and Jennifer, "There's no mistake about who's on the side of good and who's on the side of evil in this story! I remember my mom reading this to me a couple of years ago. I was a little young to understand it all, but we talked about it and I learned a lot from her."

Kerry was proud of her mom and unlike most kids her age, never missed an opportunity to compliment her. Kerry's mom was wheelchair bound, disabled with rheumatoid arthritis, and was unable to work. Mrs. Morely was famous in town despite her lack of mobility. She had a heart of gold and volunteered to open her home for church programs. Anne Morely began teaching kindergarten-aged children Bible lessons when Kerry was in that age group. Mrs. Morley was known for her mesmerizing teaching ability as well as for her oatmeal and raisin cookies which fragranced her kitchen daily and were always on a plate ready for visitors. Anne Morley loved reading aloud and had a dramatic flair that made each story come alive. She spent much time with her two daughters, pouring over storybooks from the time when Kerry and her younger sister Holly could barely focus on a page. Holly was just a year younger than Kerry and was athletic and outgoing. Kerry's dad, a firefighter for Bridgeton, kept erratic hours working long shifts to support Ann and his two daughters. Although he wished he had more "quality time," to spend with his family, he was comforted with the thought that his wife was always there for the girls. Kerry felt confident about the literature class with the principal and could hardly wait to get started. Her enthusiasm spilled over to her compatriots as they linked arms and headed for the main doors of the school.

The boys on the other hand weren't really giving literature class a second thought. They were slightly disheveled from the soccer game, which was won by Michael's team 4 to 1.

Michael lined up alongside Frank and Raffi. They were good-naturedly elbowing each other and complimenting themselves on their team's soccer victory.

"You have great ball control, Michael! You've got to play soccer more often...even join the town's junior league. What do you say?" Frank's compliment made Michael's face flush red. Frank was the local soccer star and it was unbelievable that he was sharing the limelight with Michael. "Excellent idea!" Michael laughed, but he was half serious in thinking about it for the spring.

The line of students ebbed into the school like a slowly rising tide that dissipated as lockers were filled with jackets, hats and lunch boxes and students meandered back into their home rooms for the fleeting afternoon classes. As laughing and chatting groups of friends filed into Ms. Adams' class they were struck silent at the stony face of Ms. Adam's, who was obviously highly displeased about something. Sighs erupted here and there in the room, and now and then a nervous giggle could be heard, especially among the girls. Michael noted the tense atmosphere and wondered what could be wrong. He knew that Ms. Adams was not happy about the meeting with Mr. Gladstone, but this was something else. His teacher had the look of Mt. Vesuvius prior to its devastating eruption, and most of the class looked and felt like citizens of Pompeii. Nick appeared to be the most relaxed of the whole assembled group, as if he knew exactly what was about to go down and was predicting the outcome of the blast that was imminent.

"Well, class, it seems we have a thief among us!" Ms. Adams began in a soft voice that belied her anger. She stepped away from the front of her desk and Michael immediately saw what was missing. The gasp that was sharply inhaled by most of the kids in the room indicated that they, too, took immediate notice of the missing owl ornament as well as its wrought iron perch.

"I have my suspicions about who has taken my beloved "Spooky," as Ms. Adams had nicknamed it. I can guess at the motive, but I will not make a snap judgment. I want you all to take a scrap of paper from your desk. I want you to write your name on it and fold it in half. I am going to take my biggest coffee mug and walk by each of you. I will elevate the mug so that no one need see if you drop your name into my mug or not. If you did the deed, drop your name! Obviously, it will go a lot easier on you, if you are up front with me about taking the owl ornament. Yes, you will receive a punishment of sorts, but I prefer for you to be a man, or woman, about your mistake in taking "Spooky." The loss is a class loss, not just my own personal loss. I want whoever did it to understand that."

Every face looked back at Ms. Adams with the most sincerely innocent expression that each student could muster. Michael could see the angels and demons materializing around the room. Many guardians were taking protective stances at their charge's side. Benedict was no exception. Michael looked up at Benedict's serious expression, but felt comforted by the angel's hand upon his shoulder. "Don't be afraid! The truth shall be made known in the end," Benedict whispered into Michael's ear. Jesus has told me to comfort you with that knowledge."

Ms. Adams tugged at the hem of her navy sweater tunic, pulling it down to cover more of her ample form. She hoisted the mug into the air and each student was asked to stand and place his or her hand into the mug and release their name into it if they were the guilty party. Demons rocked with mirth as she passed among the students. Some formed a procession behind her tossing blackened petals of frost bitten flowers, as if in a mock victory parade of some sort. Michael wondered if the black flower petals were real or of a spiritual nature. No one else seemed to see them, so he guessed that the janitors wouldn't need to clean up this mess.

When Ms. Adams passed by Michael he rose from his chair swiftly and plunged his fist into the mug, holding the scrap of paper with his name on it firmly in his now sweaty palm.

He breathed a sigh of relief as Maria Gracia rose next and dipped her hand in the mug in the solemn ritual that was supposed to expose the thief in the class. Michael saw Maria's eyes swimming with tears as Ms. Adams passed her by and wondered what was up. Could she be the thief or was his new friend just nervous?

Ms. Adams completed the circuit of desks and lowered the mug, covering the top of it with her hand, as if to keep unseen bugs from dropping into it. More likely her gesture was intended to keep the

24 pairs of her students' eyes from peering in and seeing something they were not supposed to see.

"Know that I will keep the name confidential and will speak to the culprit in private. I have no intention of humiliating you. We will deal with this in a professional manner." The anger in Ms. Adam's voice made everyone wonder how forgiving she would actually be once the culprit was discovered. Nick sat in his corner and was now tapping his foot impatiently, or nervously, or perhaps with a mixture of emotion. Ms. Adams uncovered the coffee mug and dipped the tip of her nose into it. Her eyes were bulging and cheeks turning bright crimson when Ms. Adams looked up at her class. Nick said in a mock whisper, " You can almost see the steam commin' from her ears!"

"O.K., no more Mr. Nice Guy as they say. I don't care if this is an invasion of privacy or not, everyone lift up the lid of your desk, I'm inspecting the contents NOW! I am swearing to the thief, whoever you are, "You will rue the day you ever decided to steal from me! I gave you a fair chance to play this out with some dignity! Now all is fair, because this is WAR!"

Ms. Adams fairly flew from desk to desk rummaging through the contents. An entourage of demons scurried in her wake. Jennifer's and Kerry's desks as well as Fawn's and surprisingly, Nick's, were so neat and orderly that one quick glance was all that was needed to see that they were not hiding stolen goods. Other desks were quite messy and required a thorough examination. Ms. Adam's rooted around in Bobby's desk for a good long time, coming up with nothing. She was irritated by the time she got to Maria Gracia, and threw a number of notebooks, stamp pads and unopened drink boxes onto the floor. This made the tears spill out of Maria's eyes and the poor girl got sympathetic looks from many of the others in the room. Michael was next and he confidently opened the top of his desk to allow Ms. Adams to rummage around. He knew that his desk was pretty messy with tons of unorganized notes he had been taking on the Arctic project spilling out of his folder in profusion. A group of illustrations Michael had been working on formed a paper tent in the valley between two piles of his many books. Ms. Adams lifted the illustration of a mother seal and its calf, which formed the tent flap covering the contents buried deeper within. Michael's expression changed from a look of patient endurance of an inconvenience to one of stricken horror as Ms. Adams triumphantly pulled the wrought iron ornament hanger from his desk.

"No it...it can't be, Ms. Adams. I...I didn't take your owl...I couldn't! I wouldn't want that creepy thing, believe me!" Michael stuttered.

Ms. Adams almost snarled her reply; "I was ready to believe you a moment ago, Michael, when you passed by the opportunity of putting your name in the cup, but no more! Class, sorry for this waste of your valuable time, but we have discovered our thief! We will deal with him after school. Michael, I want you to go to the office directly and phone home. Leave a message that you will be staying after school for one hour today to discuss this matter with me, do you understand, young man?" Ms. Adams spoke these words in a clipped tone, huffing and puffing between sentences as she was nearly hyperventilating with rage.

It was now Michael's turn to have his eyes spill over with hot tears. He was ashamed to cry in front of the class, but this unfair and untrue accusation was more than he could bear. "How could this have happened to me? How, Benedict, how? He could see Benedict's flickering form still standing at his side. The angel's expression was unreadable and this made anger spill over into Michael's words to the one he most trusted to defend him. "I thought you were guarding over me, protecting me! What happened? Where were you?" Michael whispered this last accusation in a tone that was partially heard by Maria Gracia and she cast a sorrowful look at him, as if she felt he was somehow accusing her. Michael hung his head in despair as he left the room, standing accused and accursed by his teacher and many of his fellow students. Michael glanced at Bobby as he approached the door, expecting to see sympathy and sorrow but instead he saw a look of reproach in Bobby's eyes and this above all pierced Michael's heart with a keen pain that was like that of betrayal.

Michael's mind raced with sickening thoughts, "How could Bobby believe I am guilty? I would never believe that of Bobby, even if Ms. Adam's had pulled the owl itself from Bobby's desk!

Who DID steal that blasted owl! I was framed!" Michael walked the slow walk of the condemned to the principal's office as he tried to sort through this situation and make some sense of it. What would he tell his mom and dad? Would they believe in his innocence? What punishment lay ahead? Some Christmas this was going to be!" This was the final reflection that flashed through Michael's mind before the door to the principal's office swung open.

CHAPTER 10

The form of Mr. Gladstone loomed over Michael like that of a judge looking down upon a condemned criminal. Mr. Gladstone rocked back and forth from heel to toe for several minutes before speaking. His arms were folded judiciously across his chest, resting on the polished brass buttons of his best black vest. He finally spoke in solemn tones that washed over Michael with dread.

"Michael, I am very unhappy to hear about the situation in Ms. Adams room. And frankly, I am most surprised. I never thought a young man of your character and upbringing would stoop to steal from his teacher. I know you must have done this as some misguided prank, taking the mascot of the opposition, so to speak. I advise you to make quick amends with Ms. Adams and return the owl most hastily. Things could get ugly around here if you don't. She is very, very upset with you, young man. I had to talk her out of recommending an expulsion from school."

Michael felt a lump of pain knotted in his throat, so that he couldn't even reply to Mr. Gladstone for several minutes. Suddenly, Michael was aware of Benedict standing several feet in front of him. The angel raised his strong right arm and with outstretched fingers touched Michael's belt of truth. Michael opened his mouth and said, "Well, Mr. Gladstone, I believe the Word of God when it says, 'You shall know the truth and the truth shall make you free!' That's from the gospel of John, I think. Right now I don't know the whole truth of what happened. I do know that I am not guilty, no matter how this appears to you. I did not take the owl, and I didn't take that stand and put it in my desk. That is the truth and I have faith that my speaking it will eventually set me free of this bad dream. That's what it seems to me...like one bad dream!"

Michael was shocked that he spoke so boldly and coherently to the Principal. From the look on Mr. Gladstone's face, he was shocked, too. He stood silently stroking his chin with a far off look in his eyes. Michael began to hope that Mr. Gladstone was beginning to consider the possibility that he was indeed innocent, as he had just so confidently proclaimed.

"You are a pretty unusual thief to quote the Bible as a defense. Let me think about all of this, Michael, and I will meet with you and your parents as well as with Ms. Adams directly after school. We'll see if we can sort things out. Right now you and I need to get over to the library because we are late for our first literature class on C.S. Lewis." Mr. Gladstone put his hand on the small of Michael's back as if to hurry him along. It was at once a friendly gesture, it had a calming effect on Michael so that he could stride along side the principal with his head held high, looking neither to the right nor to the left as curious students and other onlookers watched the two marching alongside each other to the library. Michael wondered what exactly was going through everyone's mind. He guessed that all of his friends and classmates had given him the thumbs down, voted him guilty without a fair trial. The thought struck him, "That's exactly what happened to Jesus! He was condemned without a fair trial, too!" Suddenly, Michael didn't really care what the rest of the school thought. He was just interested in getting to the bottom of the problem and finding the identity of the true thief.

Michael marched down the long corridor keeping stride with the principal. He was aware of Benedict's presence every step of the way, but was purposefully ignoring him. He was reluctant to give Benedict any credit for the courage he felt and the inspiration about quoting the Bible about truth, because he was still angry with him. Where was he, anyway, when the real thief was setting Michael up to be the scapegoat? Why didn't he prevent this whole mess from happening? Surely, he had the power to do that!

Mr. Gladstone deposited Michael at the library door. "Marion, get this young man eight copies of <u>The Lion, The Witch and The Wardrobe</u>, would you please?" Mr. Gladstone addressed the elderly school librarian whose pleasant bespectacled face looked down at the two of them from her elevated podium.

"Surely, Mr. Gladstone, I'd be happy to! It's a fine book! A noble book! I'm so happy you young folks are reading it!"

"No editorializing, Marion, just have Michael set up the round table in the back of the room with eight chairs and eight copies of the book, if you please." Although what Mr. Gladstone said sounded stern it was spoken with a lilting tone of voice. A wink was shared between the two, as if they were co-conspirators in a grand plot, and indeed they were, if truth were known. Both principal and librarian adored great literature and spent most free hours immersed in it. They both conspired to pass their passion along to all the students of G.W.

Marion climbed down from the elevated portion of the library and began bustling around with a sprightly air.

"Here are the books, Michael dear! Now just grab some chairs and help yourself to some bookmarks. I've been making bookmarks in my spare time for you children to use. I hope you like them!"

Michael's jaw dropped open when he drew the bookmarks out of the cardboard box Miss Marion held forth. On each colorful strip of laminated paper was a perfectly wonderful image of an angel. They weren't the chubby baby cherubs you saw at Valentine's Day. These angels were strong and fierce and powerfully glorious. Each brandished a sword and wore what looked like medieval armor. Michael swallowed loudly, gulping down some guilt as he reflected on his anger toward Benedict.

"Well, where were you, anyway?" Michael whispered aloud.

"What was that, dear?" Miss Marion queried. She had gone back to replacing some returned books on the shelves that towered over her. The tiny librarian was dragging along a small step stool with one delicate foot as she balanced a number of paperbacks in her frail arms.

"Nothing, Miss Marion. Thank you for the bookmarks. They're

awesome!" Michael was sincere in his compliment. Everyone loved Miss Marion; even the school bullies loved her. She gave everyone gifts at the holidays regardless of their reputation, and trays of homemade fudge would soon follow the bookmarks. Library was one class that tamed even the worst behaved kids. It was a school saying that the Webster's Dictionary had a picture of Miss Marion as part of the definition of the word "charming."

Michael had a bemused look on his face as he thumbed through the bookmarks. "No wonder the Christmas shepherds were so afraid when they saw the angels," Michael commented more to himself than to anyone in particular.

"Well, you don't seem very intimidated by me, Michael. I suggest you show me due respect!" Michael jumped a foot as Benedict's booming voice startled him out of his reverie.

"Some guardian you turned out to be! Why did you let this happen to me, Benedict? What's wrong with you! You let me down!" Michael was a little shocked at his own vehemence. His tone was uncharacteristically fresh with his angel friend and he began to recognize his folly when he looked into the stern visage of Benedict.

" Michael, be careful! You are speaking to a messenger of the Most High God. Do not presume that I can be taken lightly just because I care for you...more than care...I have grown to love you." Michael eyes misted over with this last confidence spoken by his angel. "I have a duty to discharge, and believe me, I take my responsibility seriously. Are you not aware of what a privilege it is for you even to see me? Very few humans have conversed with angels. Do not dishonor the favor God has bestowed upon you by being disrespectful!"

For the second time that day Michael choked back his tears. "Benedict, I am sorry for being rude to you. But I have to ask you, why didn't you stop the thief in his tracks? I know you have the power to work miracles!"

Benedict seemed to grow in stature and brilliance as he retorted, "Michael, don't you know by now that we angels don't work that way. God doesn't want us to interfere with human free will. Evil was done today, and blamed on you. I know you are innocent, but you must have faith that the Word of God is true!" Benedict was shining brightly now like a spectacular solar event. Michael averted his eyes for a moment because the glory of God was so strong on his guardian.

Michael couldn't believe that Miss Marion didn't drop all her books and come running to see the living image from her bookmarks. As a matter of fact and oddly enough the little librarian, diligent in keeping noise to a minimum in the library, didn't even seem aware of their conversation, which had become louder and more passionate in tone.

"I do have faith, Benedict, I really do!" Michael replied quite firmly and emotionally.

"Then you must believe when I tell you that God turns all things to the good for those who trust in Him...sometimes it takes a while to work out...but His promise is true! Trust in the Father, Trust in Jesus! It will all work out with the Power of the Holy Spirit on your side!" Benedict's form grew blazingly bright with these words and Michael had to cover his face. He couldn't bear to look at Benedict because it was like looking directly into the sun. When Michael did raise his eyes he was looking levelly into the face of his friend Raffi. All of the Spiritual Warfare team was now present in the library, along with Mr. Gladstone.

"Marion, would you close the library for the next forty-five minutes so that we could have some undisturbed class time?" Mr. Gladstone's query was a command rather than a question. Miss Marion didn't even blink an eye and continued to shelve books while Mr. Gladstone eyed her in disbelief. "Marion, did you hear what I just said?" The volume of the principal's voice rose dramatically. Still there was no response from the elderly staff member.

The principal rose and tapped Miss Marion on the shoulder. She jumped in fright. "Dear me, Charles, you frightened me! Why would you sneak up on an old lady like that?"

"Marion, turn on your hearing aid, please!" The principal pointed to his own ear and mimed a gesture with his fingers like turning up the dial on a radio.

"Oh, no! This is the second time this week that this contraption has shorted out on me! I'm bringing it back to the clinic and giving them a piece of my mind, even if it is almost Christmas!"

The image of Miss Marion being stern with anyone brought a smile to Michael's face. He was almost certain that her resolve to complain wouldn't last beyond the moment it was spoken. She just wasn't the complaining type. Miss Marion hobbled off to close the library for the forty-five minute class. Michael looked around the circle of his now seated comrades and he became at once disheartened. Raffi's eyes were compassionate but held a hint of sadness, as if he felt betrayed by Michael's alleged thievery.

Frank, who had recently and unofficially joined the warrior group with his stand against The Charmer series, clapped Michael on the back and whispered, "That's all right, buddy, we love you anyway." Contrary to that statement, Bobby's brown eyes shone with anger, as if he felt betrayed by Michael's supposed wrongdoing. Jennifer, Kerry, Sylvia and even Maria Gracia averted their eyes from his glance, as if they were unwilling or unable to make contact with him.

Michael never felt so alone in his life. He needed the opportunity to talk privately with his friends, but this was obviously not the time or place. All of a sudden, Michael was aware of Benedict's presence. He heard Benedict's voice and the words were spoken slowly, clearly, " I bring you Peace and Greetings from the Lord, Jesus. He is with you Michael, and will not abandon you." Benedict's words were heard as an interior voice resounding in his heart and mind, not in the usual conversational banter that Michael could hear with his ears audibly. The loneliness evaporated, and Michael was able to tune into Mr. Gladstone's lesson.

"I want you to read the first three chapters of "The Lion" tonight for homework and I want you to pay attention to the details of the setting and how the story passes from the real world into a world of fantasy and symbol. Who can tell me what I mean by the word "symbol?"

Michael's hand shot up. "Yes, Michael, what do we mean by this word?" Michael reflected for a few seconds and then answered, "A symbol is something that stands for a larger idea. Like the cross standing for the Christian faith, and like ...well, I've heard that Aslan, The Lion, is a symbol for Christ.

"Very Good, Michael, but let's not jump ahead of ourselves. We have to discover as we read if Aslan really is that, or not. Each of you keep a journal. Ask Ms. Adams for one, I know she had them handy for this unit of study on fantasy and folktales. I want you to take notes on the mythical creatures that abound in this book. The first one you meet is a faun named Tumnus.

"Besides being terribly exciting, there's a lot of humor in this book, too," noted Kerry, "If I remember correctly, Tumnus' library contains a volume entitled "Is Man A Myth?" pretty clever, huh? Kerry was warming to the topic quickly.

"It seems you've heard or read this story before, Kerry, but that's O.K. It is a great classic of literature, and you can read it over and over again, each time discovering something new and wonderful, things that you hadn't seen or understood before," Mr. Gladstone smiled benevolently at Kerry and the group.

"I don't think that's true of the Charmer books," Jennifer noted. Mr. Gladstone responded quickly and almost crossly, "We're not here to criticize The Charmer series, but to explore C.S. Lewis, I want that clearly understood!"

Jennifer meekly bowed her head and opened the book that lay on the table in front of her. The principal quickly recovered from his harsh tone and tried to make amends to Jennifer, not wanting to start the group off on the wrong footing. "That's not a bad idea, really, Jennifer. I like the fact you are opening up the work to see things for yourself. I'd like you all to open your books and began your homework assignment right now. I have a few phone calls to make; I hope you will excuse me. Our next session will be much longer and based on what you have read."

Mr. Gladstone pulled his chair back from the table and with his knees popping and cracking stood up to his full height.

"Miss Marion, you can open the doors to the library now and just keep your eyes on this group of scholars, here, that they don't get too immersed in their reading and miss math. Send them back to their room by 1:30 if you please." Marion nodded her head to the principal and went back to her task of reshelving books.

For the next half hour or so the group was absolutely silent and seemed absorbed in Lewis' world of Narnia, where the battle waged between good and evil. Then with a few minutes left Maria Gracia spoke softly. "I know that this is just a fantasy, but our real world seems locked in a battle just as intense...more so even. Michael, things look bad for you, but I just want to say that I for one don't think you took that stinking owl ornament."

Michael looked at the newest member of the group, tiny Maria who was black and beautiful. She was never more beautiful in Michael's eyes than at this moment and for the third time that day tears spilled down Michael's cheeks making slightly muddy tracks in their wake. "You're right, Maria," Michael choked out the words huskily, "I never touched that owl ornament! Someone set me up and made it look like I did it!"

"I believe you, Michael, and we'll find out who it is. I have an idea, but I can't just accuse someone without some evidence," Raffi spoke these words with kind assurance.

"I hope for your sake, and all our sakes that you are right, Michael," Bobby spoke up. "It makes all of us look real bad if you took the darned thing!"

Michael wasn't surprised by Bobby's lack of confidence in his innocence, but it hurt nonetheless. He turned to his friend and said, "I promise you that I didn't do it Bobby, and that's all I can do at this point. You either believe me or you don't!" Bobby gazed at Michael long and hard and finally lowered his eyes and said, "I give you the benefit of the doubt. After all, you haven't been proven guilty. That stand was circumstantial evidence." Everyone in the group knew Bobby loved watching courtroom dramas on TV, so his reference to circumstantial evidence didn't surprise anyone except Michael.

Jennifer was next to speak-up, "I say we stick together through thick and thin. That means that we're gonna help Michael out of this jam somehow. Michael I do hope you are telling us the truth! I want to believe you, I really do!"

"That goes for me too!" chimed in Sylvia and Kerry together. They laughed at the synchronized response and the laughter seemed to cut through the tension and pain of the moment.

The last hour and a half of class passed at a snail's pace, with withering looks given by Ms. Adams whenever she met Michael's gaze. Nick was very upbeat and more vocal than usual, especially during math class. He really wasn't half bad with calculations and had a pretty sharp mind when it came to multiplying mixed fractions.

Michael glanced at Nick often and with the compassion that God gave him, began praying silently for a breakthrough of grace. "He's really smart in some ways, Benedict. Too bad he's on the wrong side."

"God can change that, Michael," Benedict beamed, "Remember grace really is amazing! God is the God of the impossible!" Benedict's encouraging words rang in Michael's ears and he felt somehow that they applied to himself as well as to Nick.

CHAPTER 11

At exactly two-thirty, just after the dismissal bell sounded, Michael looked up from his homework notepad to lock eyes with his mother whose wounded gaze penetrated his heart. Two seconds later Michael's dad strode into the classroom, clearly irritated and agitated.

"Welcome, Mr. and Mrs. Minotti," Ms. Adams spoke with false calm and charm. "Please make yourselves comfortable in the back of the room, while I attend to bus duty." The bus duty comprised of trying to keep the lid on fourteen students from various grades as they waited for their bus number to be called over the loud speaker. Ms. Adams quickly marched the group down the hall the second the call for "bus thirteen," sounded. In just that few minutes the room was empty of all but Michael and his parents.

"Michael, we got a call from Mr. Gladstone. Can it be true? Did you steal that owl ornament from Miss Adams?" Meghan Minotti was the first to speak and her voice was infused with emotion. Michael recognized that it was very much his mother's style to get right to the point.

"I'd rather have a thief than a liar in my family, so weigh your words carefully, Michael," his dad's voice boomed loud enough for Raffi to hear as he passed the room on his way out the main exit. Raffi shot Michael a sympathetic look and gave him a thumbs-up sign. It did little to lift Michael's spirits.

"I know it looks bad for me, Mom and Dad. I have to be truthful with you. I don't know how that owl ornament stand got into my desk, but I didn't put it there, and I honestly did not take the owl. I know it seems like the kind of prank I might pull, but I did NOT do this. You just have to believe me!" The words streamed from Michael like floodwaters issuing from a broken dam. After his speech Michael buried his head in his arms and waited for a response from his parents.

"Mr. and Mrs. Minotti, I need to tell you first off that Mr. Gladstone is unable to attend our little meeting due to an emergency meeting of the budget committee. He sends his apology. I am very unhappy to have to call you to conference with me over this unfortunate situation. Michael has been against the Chad Charmer books from the start, and now this act of ...well...of sabotage, that's how I look at it. I believe that Michael took the owl ornament to demoralize the literature group that remains with me, studying the Chad Charmer book, which is a very fine and imaginative piece of literature. I really don't know what Michael and his friends have against it, or me...but this just has to stop here and now!

The words had gushed from Ms. Adams with an equally powerful pent-up force, as if she had been waiting to vent her displeasure and anger for at least several days, with no one to listen to her or sympathize. Her face had taken on a blotchy red and white coloring. The splotchy design, especially across her cheeks, appeared instantly. It looked like Ms. Adams was having an allergic reaction to the strong emotions she was experiencing.

"You're right, Ms. Adams, this does have to stop right here and now! What has to stop is this unfair judgment against our son! Yes, there is circumstantial evidence that Michael took the owl. I'll give you that. But what ever happened to a fair trial? What ever happened to a person being innocent until proven guilty?" Meghan Minotti spoke with the clarity and passion of a lawyer well versed in courtroom procedure and clearly convinced of her client's innocence.

Mr. Minotti, a bit more reserved, spoke with a momentary hesitation. "Listen, if Michael did do this thing you are accusing him of, and I tend to believe my son, because he has never...well almost never...lied to us before, he will make amends for it, I assure you. You will receive restitution for the owl if it turns out Michael took it."

"Well, thank you for that, Mr. Minotti. You are very kind to offer to pay for the owl!" Ms. Adams took the opportunity to accept the offer quickly. Repayment for the owl ornament was top priority on her list, since it was a costly investment of thirty-two dollars, not including sales tax.

"Whoa! Wait a minute! Did I say that I would pay for the owl? I did not! If Michael took it, he will have to make amends for it, and I do stress the word IF." It was now Michael's father's turn to get excited. Michael wondered in a somewhat detached manner whose face would end up the reddest hue after this passionate encounter ended.

"Well, the evidence does seem to suggest that your son is the bandit, does it not? I would also recommend that he begin earning the thirty-two dollars that it would cost me to replace my ornament. That is without the sales tax included, mind you. I was hoping to hang my owl on my holiday tree once we dismissed for the winter break."

"Ms. Adams, it wouldn't hurt Michael to begin saving some money toward possible restitution, however, I want it very clearly understood that not one red cent gets handed over until we are sure, beyond a shadow of a doubt, that the blame can be pinned on my son. Right now, I am inclined to believe that he is the scapegoat for some other culprit. I do not think Michael took it, because I believe that he is telling us the truth." Michael's dad looked exhausted from this rather long speech. Squaring off in argument against Ms. Adams was a heroic effort for Bill Minotti. He usually deferred to his wife's linguistic skills, especially if the situation involved conflict or debate of any kind. A thin line of perspiration shone on his upper lip, even though the temperature in the classroom was on the chilly side.

"You may take your son home now, but I suggest to you that you should have a good long talk with him tonight. Warn him that I will be watching him like a hawk...or maybe I should say like a snowy owl. He'd better toe the line in this room from now on!" Ms. Adams dismissed the group with a single imperious sweep of her arm. She bent over her desk and began gathering up papers and homework that she would tuck into her briefcase and carry home for correction later that evening.

Ms. Adams might be annoying and in this case very wrong, but she was a dedicated teacher used to long hours of work after the dismissal bell sent most of the G.W. faculty scurrying for their cars. It was unfortunate for her that at this point the possibility of Michael's innocence never even entered her mind. So sure was she of his guilt that she dared speak to Michael's parents in quite an alarmingly cross manner. The boldness of it all was like potent liquor to her, and she felt positively giddy as she headed for the parking lot and the one bedroom apartment she called home. Twice Ms. Adams broke into giggles while listening to the local news on her car radio, and there was absolutely nothing funny about the current outbreak of influenza.

Michael's parents, on the other hand, were dejected as they trooped down the front stairway of G.W. with their son in tow. All sorts of possibilities filled their heads, including the one horrible scenario that featured Michael guilty of theft and lying to them to get out of this jam. A light snow began to fall softly on the dispirited family as they approached the street parking where Michael's parents had abandoned their Chevy in haste. The sharp north wind had picked up and a parking ticket flapped from the windshield wiper blade on the driver's side of the car.

"Great, this is just great! Merry Christmas from the town of Bridgeton! Meghan, I gave you a quarter for the meter, what happened?" Mr. Minotti grumbled loudly over the rising wind.

"I should have given that woman a piece of my mind! How dare she speak to us in such imperious tones. She has absolutely overlooked the other possibilities in this situation, don't you think so, Bill?" Meghan looked tentatively at her husband, hoping to deflect his angry outburst about the parking ticket and refocus it on the true culprit, Ms. Adams.

"Mom and Dad, I know that this looks bad, really bad for me, but you've got to believe me, I did not do this! Benedict promises me that the truth will come out in the end. I really believe he will help me. He never lets me down!" Michael managed to give his speech before his dad even turned over the engine of the car.

"Who the heck is Benedict? How is this kid going to help you when your parents aren't even sure how to handle this situation! I think I'll speak with Mac in the morning and get some good legal advice from him," his mother concluded with a far away look in her eyes.

"I've been meaning to tell you about Benedict. He's my guardian angel, and I know it sounds wild, but I can see and hear him most of the time. Not all of the time, but he usually appears when I need him the most and he gives me good advice and courage from the Lord. Benedict is awesome, and if he is working on my side, I know this will turn out all right."

Bill and Meghan Minotti were stunned speechless. Their mouths were open and their eyes were large round saucers reflecting the gathering storm outside. Michael's mother was the first one to break the silence, "Michael, whatever do you mean? You don't really believe you are having actual conversations with this angel person, Benedict, do you?" It was hard for her to keep the edge of anxiety from creeping into her voice. This was the icing on the cake, so to speak. First there was the call at work from the principal with the horrible news that Michael was being accused of theft, then the nasty confrontation with Ms. Adams and now this nonsense from Michael. It was almost too much for a mother to bear. While she was contemplating this thought, the first tears of this awful day sprung into her eyes. Meghan wiped them away quickly, hoping no one would notice.

"Michael, don't add this wild yarn about an angel named Benedict to your story! It does NOT help your case one iota with me, you understand?" Bill Minotti cranked the volume up one more notch to register his mounting anger.

"Don't worry, I won't mention Benedict again to you, either of you. But it doesn't make him any less real or any less of a help to me! Right now, and I know it's not nice to say this, but I feel Benedict is helping more than either of you are! At least he knows the truth and believes in me. I don't think either of you really do believe me!"

"That's quite enough, Michael! Your mother and I need some time to ourselves to digest all of this. We are on your side, whether you think so or not. Let's just head home, have supper, and get some much-needed rest. While we figure out how to handle all of this, you meet your responsibilities, which are homework, chores and earning a little extra money in case it is needed to repay Ms. Adams. Now if you don't mind, let's travel the short distance home in silence. I need to think and to concentrate on the slippery pavement!" Michael's father spoke with authority and the car grew quiet. Each fell into their own thoughts as they rode the half-mile to the little ranch house. The sight of the snow carpeting the lawn and making the neighborhood Christmas lights sparkle in icy reflections did nothing to excite the Minotti family as they approached home.

Each member lumbered from the car with burdens of doubt and sorrow on their shoulders. They ate in relative silence, which was broken by mundane phrases like, "Please pass the salt," or "Get your homework done now!" spoken mostly by Michael's folks.

At last, Michael's eyes were shut after the briefest of prayers that took the form of the prayer most often heard in heaven: "Jesus, help me! Amen!" The powerful turmoil that surrounded Michael all day had taken its toll and he readily fell into a deep sleep, which enveloped him like a bank of fog. It was a dreamless sleep, yet it was not without the comforting sense of Benedict's faithful presence and the Lord's unfailing love.

While Ms. Adams sipped a small glass of sherry and finished correcting the mixed fraction quiz, (not without errors on her part) Michael's parents turned to one another with questions that seemed unanswerable, and a fear that pressed into their hearts and minds with an almost unbearable weight.

"Bill, do you think our son has had a nervous breakdown of some sort? First this accusation about stealing, and now his crazy talk about an angel, named Benedict, no less!"

"Meghan, I hate to admit it, but I am wondering about our son's sanity, too. I mean it's not that I don't believe in angels. I guess I do. They are in the Bible here and there. But they just don't appear to regular people in this day and age! Do they?"

Benedict, who had slipped from Michael's side momentarily to witness this conversation, began to shake his head in disbelief and sorrow. "If they only knew the truth of it!" Bill and Meghan's guardian angels exchanged glances that spoke of discouragement. Benedict's countenance and expression changed to calm confidence and firmness. He drew himself up to his full and massive height "Don't get depressed by this talk, both of you look sharp! You have a lot of protection and guidance to give! Start whispering encouragement to these poor folks!" Benedict was in charge, clearly outranking the other guardian angels by his status and authority.

Before angel or parent could speak another word a loud and repeated moaning could be heard from the general direction of Michael's bedroom. Although it sounded remarkably like Michael's voice, Benedict knew in an instant that it was coming from a mimicking spirit sent to mock Michael. Benedict arrived with his broad shield flashing and commanded the small dark entity to get out NOW in the name of the Lord. It tumbled backward out the unopened window, but not before sending shivers down the spines of Michael's parents with a piercing scream that was truly identical to Michael's most horrified call for help. The shock of the sound awakened Michael and he sat bolt upright from his pillow. Benedict was regretting not commanding silence from the little spirit before he sent it scrambling into the night.

"Michael, it's all right, we're here!" Meghan and Bill pushed through the narrow bedroom doorway together. Bill knelt beside the bed while Meghan sat by Michael's side on the crumpled comforter that had been automatically thrown off with Michael's alarmed awakening.

"Was that me?" Michael questioned. It sounded like himself upon awakening but Michael had no conscious awareness of making any noise.

"No, it was NOT you so don't get excited!" Benedict breathed into his ear and calm was restored to Michael's system.

"Michael, dear, you have been through a lot today. I'll tell you what, let's pray together for the Peace of Christ to come into this home tonight," Michael's dad spoke these comforting words and led the family in prayer, "Father, this is a dark and troubling time for our family and especially for our Michael. Shed your light of truth on this situation and restore peace and harmony in our family. We ask this in the name of the Prince of Peace, Your Son, Jesus. Amen."

A hush fell over the family and Benedict overspread the threesome with a covering of his mighty wings. "You will be protected from the evil one's plans and victory will be yours. Truth will be your vindication and love will conquer all in this season of love. Christmas Blessings and an extra measure of grace fall upon you now and remain with you!" Benedict spoke these words that only Michael could hear as an answer to his dad's prayer. "Benedict says that our prayers will be answered. I guess we just have to be patient," Michael responded dreamily. He shut his eyes and began to drift back to sleep.

Somewhere just outside Michael's door, he was aware of his parents muffled voices. As he drifted off to sleep he could hear them discussing which child psychiatrist they should take Michael to in order to, "get over this angel thing and to get to the bottom of the owl business." Oddly enough it made Michael laugh to himself. It was a strange reaction, really. He should be disappointed but he wasn't. Even knowing that his parents did not believe him about Benedict did not prevent Michael's descent into a peaceful sleep.

"Benedict, you are so huge and so powerful, it's really funny that they can't see you! You take up so much space when you materialize. You have to put up with so much doubt and disbelief from us humans! Poor Benedict!" Michael sank deeper into slumber and remained covered by the protective wings of his great friend until dawn spilled its golden light onto Michael's face.

CHAPTER 12

Across town Nick was waking up. He had spent an almost sleepless night gazing into a crystal positioned above his prized stolen possession. Glassy eyed and murmuring to the silvery figure, Nick spent hours trying to communicate with the spirit infesting the owl ornament. Finally, in the wee hours of the morning the white-cloaked demon appeared in a shimmering vision that left Nick wild eyed and quite shaken. Nick was in total awe of the majestic appearance of this horned 'owl god,' who seemed the embodiment of wisdom itself. He felt honored to be able to ask its advice on the small matter of revenge against the one person Nick felt that he hated. That one person was, of course, Michael Minotti.

The owl demon silently held Nick's gaze for many minutes during which time Nick became deeply entranced, his own will diminished as he became yoked to this nasty spirit. He was told by a bird-like voice the necessary items he needed to procure in order to perform the ceremony to weaken Michael and to destroy his reputation. Nick needed to get his hands on one of Michael's school notebooks, and also a lock of Michael's hair. "How am I going to do that?" Nick questioned.

An instant rebuke came in the form of a severe pain in his forehead. The owl's talons gripped onto him like a vise. The searing pain sent Nick cringing to his knees. "Sorry, I'll just do it! Don't worry! I'll get the items!" Nick cried as the pain lifted from his brow. The owl screeched, a hideous half mocking laugh, half cry of triumph and with wings beating like those of a crazed insect; it disappeared into the night. Nick sensed that it hadn't gone far, and knew that he was right when he looked into the eyes of the glass ornament that hung on a wrought iron hook above his night table. The same potent eyes stared back at Nick and sent him stumbling heavily to his bed to sleep a dreamless sleep. It was as if Nick had tumbled into a black hole in deep space and became absorbed by the magnitude of its gravity. He was powerless on his own to escape from the plans set before him, plans to soothe his jealousy, dark plans for vengeful witchcraft.

That same night, in one of the loveliest and largest mansions in Bridgeton, Fawn Wainwright sat on a pile of pillows in her ivory and purple bedroom pouring over the Chad Charmer book she had brought home. She skipped over whole chapters, her long white fingers skimming over pages of print, seeking the page that gave the name of the potion that transferred skills from one person to another, and that magically bonded one person to another, making them submissive to the spell caster's will. She cried aloud when she found the name and description for the Potion of Pandora. She was eager to find the ingredients listed for this elixir and she knew exactly where to put her hands on it. On the highest shelf of the mahogany bookcase in her father's study sat the leather bound edition of The Complete Compendium of Spells and Potions, easily the largest tome in his occult collection. Fawn's plan was to concoct the brew herself. She had formed the intention to share it with Jennifer, thereby linking Jennifer to her forever. She would possess all of the qualities that made Jennifer popular and pretty. Jennifer would be Fawn's shadow, enthralled by her, forever her friend, but always subservient to Fawn's queenly ways. Fawn practiced "white witchcraft," convincing herself that what she wished and "spelled" for herself and for others was not evil, not harmful, but really for the best for everyone concerned. She was undeniably the one destined to be a leader in the class, and Fawn knew that she would rule wisely and well.

Fawn's eyes widened with wonder as she found the brew listed in the Chapter of the Charmer book entitled, " Forming Friends in a

Frightful Manner." Grabbing a purple notebook, Fawn propped herself against a stack of pillows and began laboriously copying the name of the potion and tips on how to manipulate people into believing her, even when caught in a lie. She noted how "lying when convenient or caught in a compromising situation," ranked high among the skills promoted in this chapter.

Tiptoeing down the hall past a vacant guest bedroom, Fawn slid noiselessly by the room sometimes occupied by her older sister Astral and exhaled loudly once she was inside the handsome study and library that belonged to her dad. She didn't even realize that she had been holding her breath until the moment she was safely inside the library. Her parents wouldn't be too pleased with her prowling around in the wee hours of the morning on a school night. Luckily, Astral was between high school and college, taking a year off to explore Europe. Astral would have caught Fawn and would have happily turned her in for breaking the rules. "Chad always breaks the rules and no one seems to care much that he does. I'd like to be more like him!" Fawn whispered to herself. Fawn's parents had indulged in a little brandy "nightcap," and were snoring soundly several floors below. Fawn was glad that no one was likely to see or hear her as she slid the heavy tome off the shelf. It landed with a thud on the polished desk beneath the book stacks.

Fawn slipped her notebook and pen out from a voluminous pocket in her purple satin robe. "No, it's best I bring everything back to my room where I can be comfortable!" It wasn't easy juggling the huge book, notebook, feathered pen and several smaller reference books on spells, but Fawn managed to sneak back to her room in near perfect silence. Ensconced again on several large pillows, Fawn found the proper index and swiftly found the potion that the Charmer book referenced. "It's all here, just as I knew it would be! The books may be fiction, but a lot of research went into them, that's for sure!" Fawn noted. Her parents wouldn't approve of Fawn delving into the "Craft" at this high level, but her hero Chad Charmer often went beyond safe limits into areas and things labeled "dangerous," by adults. Fawn felt justified in doing so as well. After all, she had a good cause! As she concentrated on getting an exact listing of ingredients, a pasty faced wraith clung to her shoulder spurring her on to new heights of imagination. "Goodness, I wonder if I'll be able to skate like Jennifer after sharing this potion with her!"

The thin, pale demon giggled in delight and quoted a tawdry Hollywood star of yesteryear, who was noted for saying, "Goodness has nothing to do with it, sweetheart!" The demon meant that with every twisted element of its being, relishing the plans for harm that grew with every new jot and line on Fawn's notebook page.

With practiced stealth, Fawn dimmed her bedroom light when she heard her parent's footfall on the hallway staircase. They hesitated briefly at the top of the stairs; Fawn noted to herself that they were probably checking to see if her room was suitably darkened and quiet. It seemed to her that they must have been convinced that their daughter was fast asleep because the sound of their footsteps continued down the long marble hallway to the isolated master suite that overlooked the gardens and the pool.

Fawn tiptoed down the same sweeping spiral of stairs just a few moments after hearing the door close to her parent's suite of rooms. Fawn threw on the lights illuminating the deck that swept past the breakfast nook toward the mudroom. Outside the kitchen window Fawn could see enormous snowflakes falling majestically from a black velvet canopy of night sky. She lit two scented jar candles and set them on the peninsula. An aroma of spicy pumpkin and nutmeg wafted from the thick brown pots and enveloped Fawn in a dreamy, cozy warmth. The green marble top of the peninsula was cleared of earlier debris from holiday baking. It was a convenient spot for Fawn to gather the small porcelain jars containing the ingredients she had copied into her journal. One item was missing when exhaustion overtook her. "I'll worry about that in the morning," she murmured to herself.

Trudging up the staircase again, Fawn was aware of the sighing of the wind as it swept through the skeletal branches beyond the bay windows on the landing. She paused for a moment and gazed out at the storm, pleased that she was safe and warm inside her little palace. Suddenly Fawn envisioned the pale spirit of envy reflected in the glass pane above her head. Its eyes were hypnotic and cold.

Fawn rubbed her face with the back of her hand, hoping to clear her vision. The demon had vanished, but she was left with these thoughts, "You're not anything like Jennifer. You will never be! She'll never even give you the time of day! Nothing will ever change...unless you follow through with that brew! You've got to do it, girl! You owe it to yourself!"

"What do I have to be jealous about? I'm the wealthiest, luckiest girl in that whole school," Fawn sniffed, "and soon I'll be the most popular, too!" She returned to her bedroom with renewed determination to finish what she had started. It was just a sweep of the minute hand shy of two o'clock in the inky blackness of early morning that Fawn finally fell asleep with pen in hand, her cheek pressed into the page of potion and spell that she had meticulously hand copied. At the bottom of the page she had just written the words, "Let it be done! Let the charm enchant!"

CHAPTER 13

Michael woke up and propped one arm on the side of the bed to glance at the clock. He fell back on his pillow to sleep an additional fifteen minutes before the alarm rang. An intense dream filled his sleeping mind with images of swordplay. He was wielding the angelic sword of truth that Benedict had given him, cutting through an intense darkness that was filled with sinister and cunning enemies. Michael's blade was sharp and true and wherever it sliced a brilliant light pierced through the heavy shadows routing the enemy and illuminating the path that Michael was to take. He strode out of the dream and into fresh morning light and a state of heightened consciousness that informed him that this recent dream, symbolic of his situation, was true in a very real sense. He would use the Word of God and Truth as his weapon in the days ahead, and this sword would not fail him; it would free him!

"Good morning, Benedict!" Michael spoke to the shimmering image of his friend that was barely visible in the white dawn of this Friday morning. "I hope the Lord takes this the right way when I say 'thank God it's Friday!" because I mean it from the bottom of my heart!" Benedict's form took on solid definition and his brilliant grin was far brighter than the snowy landscape just outside Michael's window.

"I think God knows exactly what you mean! It hasn't been easy the past couple of days and I can't promise you anything better until the Truth wins, Michael, but know this: the Truth will win! I am confident of it. The Lord has spoken that you will be victorious in the end. So be calm and face the enemy without fear. He is nothing in comparison to the might and will of the Lord!" Together Michael and Benedict began praying on the whole armor of God. With the helmet of salvation Michael prayed for the gift of discernment so that he could recognize truth from lies and identify evil spirits by name.

Michael prayed for the compassionate heart of Jesus with the breastplate of righteousness. "Let me love you above all, dear Lord...and my neighbor as myself." The familiar golden rule took on a new depth of meaning when Michael was reminded by Benedict that his neighbor included Nick and Fawn as well as other kids that had sided with the so called white witches and Nick's "darker power," at school. Michael knew that the battle was not against them, but against the evil spiritual forces that had a stronghold in his classroom with the presence of that book.

The belt of truth shone with a golden brilliance this morning and Michael knew that it would play an important part in the victory over evil. The shoes of the Gospel of peace looked more and more like combat boots.

Benedict encouraged Michael by saying, " When the war is over, true peace will be restored!" Benedict held Michael's shield of faith, telling him, "I have it ready for you, depend on God in all situations, He will never abandon you, Michael! It will stave off the fiery darts sent by the evil one in battle situations!"

A strong scabbard attached to the belt of truth held the Sword of the Spirit, which is the Word of God. It was gleaming, ready for battle, a mighty weapon more powerful than the legendary swords carried by King Arthur and the Knights of the Round Table. While Michael and Benedict concluded by praising and worshipping God, the golden glory, the rare atmosphere of heaven, began filtering down covering Michael's back so that he would not be taken by surprise by the enemy. The Lord God was making sure Michael was fully dressed for warfare, for He alone truly knew what momentous events were about to take place.

"Michael, are you awake?" You can take your time this morning, there's a one-hour delayed opening of school due to the snow we got last night. It was just seven inches, but was enough to keep the school buses from leaving until the lot gets plowed and shoveled free!" Michael heard his mom's voice just outside his bedroom door.

Despite the delayed opening, Michael was up and dressed in his warmest flannel shirt and favorite woolen sweater and out the door before greeting his father. Mr. Minotti was still upstairs preparing for a sales presentation to be given in the western part of the state later in the afternoon. It was okay with Michael that he didn't get a proper send off from his folks, simply because he felt a lingering hurt and knew he would behave awkwardly around them. He remembered their doubts and disbelief surrounding the theft of the owl and the reality of Benedict, and that alone stung his insides more than the sharp wind that had picked up out of the north.

The sky was a deep electric blue that seemed to Michael to be unique to the morning after snowstorms. He picked up his pace to school despite the beauty of the crystalline world that met his wandering eyes. It appeared as if clumps of frozen popcorn clung to branches and power lines. Overnight God had made a wonderland of nature and technology alike. Wreaths and evergreen trimmings were thick with sparkling ermine edges. As the sun reflected off the snow crystals making them dazzling mirrors of its energy, Michael thought about how each Christian was supposed to reflect Jesus to the world in just the same way.

It was a pretty profound thought that made him feel slightly amazed. "Thank you, Jesus, for reminding me that I am supposed to bring your light wherever I go. Amen." Benedict smiled widely as he watched Michael's prayer ascend to the throne room of heaven.

Sally's Bakery was just one storefront prior to the stationary shop, which displayed the Chad Charmer ornaments. The sweet laden bow window invited Michael to pause, intrigued by the display of danish and donuts piled onto ruby red platters. Each plate towered with confections and sprigs of holly and Michael engaged in deciding which looked more delicious, the raspberry twists frosted with sugar or the fat Bismarck donuts loaded with whipped cream and cherry jelly. The comforting treats literally beckoned him to enter for a preschool indulgence. Aromas of hot chocolate, cinnamon and freshly baked breads formed an almost visible steamy hook that latched onto Michael's jacket and pulled into the dimly lit interior of the shop.

Benedict smiled indulgently at Michael as he bent over to look into the glass case of baked goods. The plump Bismarck chosen almost made the angel wish for a moment that he were able to taste this goody with a human tongue.

Brass bells latched to the entry to Sally's tinkled causing the angel and his charge to turn and see a scowling Nick, the next customer to enter the tiny shop. How the sight and scent of such delicious wonders could possibly be met with an angry expression was beyond both Benedict and Michael.

"G'morning, Nick, I see you couldn't resist the window display either," Michael ventured in a friendly fashion. "I don't see anything good about this morning, and I'm here for a fix of hot chocolate. Didn't get much sleep last night." Nick wondered why he was so wordy with this nemesis of his. As he saw it, Michael was, after all, the cause of his sleepless night.

While Michael paid for his donut, Nick ordered his hot chocolate with lots of whipped cream and three sugars to make it extra sweet. The thin bakery clerk stuck out her spidery arm in front of Nick's nose and pointed to the back shelf of the shop. "Help yourself to sugar packets, napkins and spoons, Hon," she spoke in a hoarse voice that suggested years of cigarette smoking. Nick turned and grabbed a handful of white sugar packets and jammed them into his jacket pockets.

Michael caught a glimpse of a shiny silvery object nestled in the inner pocket of Nick's jacket and it was enough to knock the wind out of him. He had suspected Nick's involvement in the theft of the owl ornament, but now he was certain. "Tell me, Nick, why did you take Ms. Adam's ornament? Was it just to get me in trouble or what?" Michael spoke boldly and he was aware of Benedict's protective presence.

"What are you talkin' about? Man, you must be dreamin'. I thought I was tired, but you are definitely sleepwalking!" Nick tried to bluster his way out of the dilemma. He wasn't quite sure why he was feeling guilty suddenly. He hadn't felt at all bad about what he had done up to this point. It was totally justified in his mind. It was a perfect plot to revenge himself on this little nerd, Michael, and he was not going to let stupid guilt feelings ruin his plan to be top dog in Ms. Adams class. Besides, Chad Charmer played a similar trick on his archrival Kent Tremblay III in volume three of the Chad Charmer series, Dark Raiders of the Night. "My motto is if it's OK with Chad, its OK with me!" Nick spoke this last thought aloud in a half whisper.

"Nick, I don't know why you did it, but I know you did. Moreover, I can see that nasty owl demon perched on your shoulder. It's got quite a talon hold on you!" Michael could see the demon quite clearly now, as it glared in his direction, snapping its beak like mouth within inches of Michael's face. Michael flinched and took a step back from Nick and in that instant Benedict's sword leapt into his hand. Michael stated boldly, "The truth shall set you free," and the sword, which remained invisible to all but Michael, the angels and demons that were present, grew bright. Michael instinctively made a thrust toward the owl demon. The move was swift and direct, hitting the dark agent directly on its chest. Angels cheered as the winged beast went flying against the wall and then sprawled on the floor where Michael trampled it underfoot.

Nick was temporarily disarmed. He felt a keen longing to be like Michael, not against him. Tears that welled from an inexpressible longing flooded to his eyes. Nick swiped at them with embarrassment. Michael reached deep within his pocket and grabbed a handful of Kleenex. His mom was always filling jackets with tissue provision during the cold winter months. He stretched out his hand toward the thief who had been determined to ruin his reputation. He wasn't sure why, but Michael suddenly was overwhelmed by a feeling of compassion for his enemy. Nick grabbed several tissues and blew his nose loudly.

Quietly and firmly Michael spoke, "Nick, I am praying for you and I won't stop until you are claimed for Christ!" A flicker of hope lit Nick's eyes and a shudder went through his body. Immediately, the demon rose from the floor and fixed his demented eyes on Nick. Hypnotized by the cobra-like stare of his enemy, Nick hardened his heart once more.

Nick fairly shouted at Michael, "You know you are crazy, man!

I don't know what that was all about! I think I'm catching a flu bug! Hey, weren't you just out sick? I'm keepin' away from you...probably got a fever and you're seeing things."

Nick turned to leave the store and as he pocketed a fistful of sugar packets Michael could see the owl demon rise from the floor and fly once more to Nick's shoulder. Once settled, the demon dug in its talons. Michael could see Nick wince with pain and the shoulder carrying the demonic burden slumped under the weight of jealousy, bitterness and witchcraft.

The momentary vulnerability left Nick's eyes as he turned to issue a whispered curse. Benedict lifted Michael's shield of faith and the curse deflected harmlessly, falling to the muddy floor.

Nick glared at Michael with hatred and pronounced, "You better go home and stay home if you know what's good for you!" Michael noted how Nick's voice had changed taking on the rasping birdlike quality of the demon he carried so close to his heart. The look in Nick's eyes was icier than the temperature outside. He flung open the door and tramped onto the frozen sidewalk, moving swiftly in the direction of G.W.

Michael felt like a seasoned soldier and the first skirmish of the day encouraged him. The glowing sword was once again sheathed at his side, ready for further combat. He tucked his donut into his backpack for later and headed out the door into the brisk north wind.

"Benedict, I saw hope in Nick's eyes. It was just for a few seconds after your sword flattened the enemy. I believe we can reclaim Nick for the kingdom of our Lord. What do you think?"

"I think I am very proud of you, my friend! Most every other human I have known and guarded would be furious with their rival. You surprise me, Michael! You pleasantly surprise me! Yes, I do believe that Nick can and should be sought after as a trophy for Jesus in this ugly war. Keep focused on Jesus and watch out for the enemy agents...the lies, the witchcraft, the jealousy, the bitterness and especially revenge which would try and attach itself to you!

"The compassion I prayed for this morning when I prayed on the breastplate of righteousness is real, Benedict, I can feel it in my heart and it is protecting me against wanting revenge. I just want to let the truth be known by everyone, especially by Ms. Adams and

Mr. Gladstone. How do I do that so that they really believe me? How do I let them know Nick is the thief without losing Nick forever to the enemy?"

"If I knew the answer to that one, I would be more than an angel, Michael, and I am not...but I do know that God is on our side and if God is for us, who can be against us? No one of much importance! Right?"

Michael grinned with renewed confidence and gave Benedict a high five as he shouted into the clear morning air, "Right!"

CHAPTER 14

On the other side of town Leo Wainwright was driving his daughter to school in their shiny new black BMW. Fawn had dark smudges under her eyes to give witness to the nearly sleepless night she had spent. She had gladly given the better part of her night to pouring over directions and gathering ingredients required for the magic potion she and Jennifer would soon consume.

After a bare two hours of sleep, in the wee hours of the morning, Fawn began her brew with apple cinnamon tea and honey, a harmless base. Because her parents were heavily into the craft most of the needed ingredients had been available to Fawn, and were lined up in small porcelain jars on the counter top. Fawn followed the text of the The Complete Compendium of Spells and Potions with precision. With the addition of each herb, Fawn whispered parts of the spell, which she believed would bind Jennifer's soul to hers, and transfer all of the popular girl's talents and friendships to Fawn.

One thing was missing, the berry of a particular flower common to springtime gardens. Fawn, in desperation, had substituted a handful of bright red berries she picked out of a floral centerpiece in the Wainwright dining room. Luckily, the Wainwrights were having members of their coven over to dinner on Saturday evening to celebrate Winter Solstice. This was one of the group's favorite holidays celebrating the shortest daylight hours of the year and the imminent return of the sun.

Deep in the darkest December hours Fawn had labored with a horde of demons hovering around her gloating over the work of black magic that was afoot. As she added the two dozen or so crimson berries to the steaming concoction Fawn concluded the spell. She had just the slightest nagging doubt that the substituted berries would break the potent effect of the brew. She relished the intoxicating aroma of the "tea," she had prepared and poured it into an earthenware pitcher to cool slightly.

"Oh spirit of this spell, I wish I could see you!" No sooner had Fawn spoken these words aloud than a faint glimmer appeared in the air by the small brick oven and chimney that was central to the kitchen. "I see you over by the hearth! Oh, do materialize for me!" Fawn breathed. For just a fleeting moment Fawn could see the most gorgeous fairy like creature, pale and thin and delicate with golden hair streaming down covering her tiny feet. "Oh, you are beautiful!" Fawn exclaimed.

"As beautiful as you will soon be, my child," spoke the apparition. As it smiled, tiny wolf like teeth appeared behind the full ruby lips. Fawn rubbed her eyes because the teeth were frightening her and didn't seem to match the rest of the enchanting vision she had just seen. When she opened her eyes again, the spirit had vanished.

As Fawn rode in silence to school, her liquid magic was now contained in an insulated thermos clutched to her chest. She pondered the mystery of the gorgeous spirit of the spell that she was certain she had seen and heard from in the dawning hours of this new day.

Her father's voice broke into her reverie; "Moonbeam, my sweet, your mother and I are going shopping tonight for the festivities tomorrow. Would you like to join us? We'd like to treat you to a few Solstice gifts at the mall. Your grades have been quite good and we are very proud of you!" Fawn's father spoke in a rich baritone and the promise of shopping together with her parents after school excited Fawn more than usual. She would need new clothes, after all, to match her new image. Fawn's grin spread as she realized that she would soon be looked upon as the most popular girl in her class.

"Yeah, dad, that would be awesome! You bet I'll join you. We'll have quite a celebration on Saturday, won't we!" Fawn responded warmly. Lilith and Leo Wainwright always threw quite a wonderful Winter Solstice party with blazing Yule log, loads of delicacies and desserts, and plenty of grog. Unfortunately, most of the adults consumed too much grog and other heady liquors, with a few needing to spend the overnight at "The Manor," as their home was called.

"Be ready to head out by dark, hon. We'll grab a bite at the Jungle Cafe and see about those gifts. Your mom and I are leaving work early this afternoon to pick up the liquor and check with the caterer. Hope you have an idea what you want to buy so we can get home and get rested for Solstice." Fawn's dad finished his speech with a mysterious lilt to his voice as he pronounced the name of the pagan feast day. He chuckled to himself, thinking of some mischievous pranks to pull on his coven cohorts as they drove up to the curb in front of G.W. "We'll have to make a quick visit to the magic and joke shop, honey! Don't forget we want to make an early start!"

"I'll be waiting with that wish list in my hot little hands, don't worry about that!" Fawn smiled a pale smile and hopped out of the Beemer nearly loosing her footing on the icy sidewalk. She skidded into Nick as he turned into the walkway in front of the school.

"Oh, it's only you!" Nick brushed at his black leather jacket as if to shake off the contact with Fawn.

"You won't be saying that after today!" Fawn corrected him with a tinge of bitterness in her voice.

"What do ya mean by that? Have some dark secrets, do ya?" Nick responded sensing a kindred spirit in Fawn. Indeed the green-eyed demon of jealousy dwelt in them both. Dark sparks, like the negative image of lightning, flew from their eyes as they looked at each other. Without exchanging explanations, both had an instant "knowing" that they were similarly engaged in some heavy magic, driven by forces unseen and frightening.

"I'll let you in on my little "dark secret," if you must know. Last night I followed the recipe for the spell Charmer cast on Willy Wiggins...you know...Pandora's Potion! I was nearly perfect in replicating it. The only problem was that I couldn't find one ingredient. However, I substituted quite brilliantly, but I'm not sure that it will be as potent a mix."

Directed by the owl demon's inspiration, Nick improvised with a lie, just a small one, to build his reputation. "My little Fawn, you need my help. I have a potent ingredient to add to your brew. One that will seal the magic perfectly and make it stick forever. See me at recess by the fence and bring an audience of your closest friends to help with the incantation. Who are you casting this on? No, let me guess! It must be one of Michael's silly little friends...one of the Warriors of God!" Nick was surprised at these last words, because he never had thought of them as such. The evil spirit with him identified Michael's group accurately and gave voice to their true identity with much disdain. "Let's see...is it Little Warrior Kerry? Jennifer or Sylvia? My guess is that it's Miss Popularity herself, Jennifer. Am I right?"

Fawn looked at Nick oddly, a little shaken by his accurate pinpointing of her little scheme. "Yes, it's Jennifer, and I'll BE her in just a little while. Not that I want to be a God's Warrior, or whatever it was you called her."

"I'll see you in just a few short hours to seal the deal, Fawn. Just remember who got you to the top of the heap when you reap the benefits of this little spell!" Nick grinned widely at the grand plan he had just launched: get rid of that little twerp, Michael and get in with the in crowd at last! Yes, everything was shaping up exactly according to his hopes and plans. Nick hardly noticed the painful twinge in his shoulder from the talons of the occult owl demon that had latched onto him. He hardly noticed that he was walking with a heavier burden of lies and deceit as he entered the school on that last Friday before Christmas on the eve of the darkest day of the year!

Michael approached the school a few minutes after Nick and Fawn entered the building. He sensed the heaviness in the atmosphere surrounding G.W. and instinctively knew that something evil was afoot. It wasn't instinct really, it was the Holy Spirit letting him know that he should be on guard against attacks from the enemy, and to discern situations and places well before entering into what could hurt or harm him.

"Benedict, I could feel afraid of what I am sensing, but instead I feel at Peace. Odd, isn't it? I've never been in so much trouble in my life, but I feel very calm and certain that the Lord is in charge, and everything is gonna be all right!"

Benedict grinned and gave Michael an encouraging pat on the back. "Don't forget that the Lord gives Peace that surpasses understanding. That means that our heads tell us that we should be upset by circumstances, but our hearts are at rest and we can even laugh at the plots and plans of the enemy because we truly know who WINS in the end. All of the time!" Benedict's image became transparent to Michael, and then vanished, but the power of his words remained behind.

"Hey, Michael, wait up for me!" Raffi's voice rang out in the crisp morning air and it filled Michael with warmth and happiness at the mere sound of it.

"Hey, Raffi, you and me are still best buds, right?" Michael spoke with confidence.

"I'd never let weird stuff like what's been happening in Ms. Adam's class keep me from being friends with you, Michael. You know that. I don't believe for a minute that you stole that nasty owl. Maybe you'd want to smash it to smithereens, like I do, but you wouldn't do anything dishonest. You love the Lord too much for that!"

"Thanks, Raffi, your vote of confidence means a lot to me!" Michael choked out the words, suddenly overcome with grateful emotion. "Even people who love the Lord a whole lot sometimes do stuff that they shouldn't. That's why confession is so good for the soul, but in this case, I've got to say I'm totally not guilty!"

"You know the others have faith in you, too. Oh, Bobby took a little convincing, but he believes in you, too. He originally thought you took that owl to trash it, but knowing how repulsive it is to you, well, he's willing to give you the benefit of the doubt. Honestly, I think Bobby is a little jealous of your gift of seeing the Spirit World, you know. Having a real face-to-face relationship with your guardian angel is pretty amazing! He thinks it's a little unbelievable but I think you've convinced him. I don't know if I'd want to see my angel if it meant I had to see the enemy spirits, too. Doesn't that frighten you?"

"If I doubted for a moment that the Lord is totally, awesomely more powerful, then I would be afraid," Michael asserted. "Benedict reminds me daily of his great care for me. I am not in this alone, and the battle belongs to the Lord. Really all I have to do is take a stand for the truth and in the end, I just stand still and watch it happen! I pray for the grace not to fall on my head with this one, not to crumble or grumble or give in to the lies, name-calling, threats or bullying. Raffi, I have to admit to you that I am getting sick and tired of this and I am looking forward to getting out for Christmas vacation next Tuesday. Too bad we have to go back to school next week at all. I sure could use the break!"

Raffi didn't say anything in response, but put his arm around Michael's shoulder as they entered the building together. That comradely gesture said it all to Michael, and gave him the lift he needed to enter Ms. Adams class with his head held high despite the stares and whispers that accompanied the terrible passage to his desk in the back of the room.

Nick spoke in a stage whisper that could be heard by most of the kids in the class, "Well, if it isn't the owl- snatcher himself. Mr. Goody Two Shoes gets caught in the act of bird napping! Ha-ha-ha!" The mocking laughter took on the tone of the owl demon itself, and ended in a sound that was more like a shrieking hoot than a laugh. Several kids turned and stared at Nick with looks that spoke volumes about their discomfort with the sounds that issued from his throat. Fawn hissed to Nick, "Be quiet before you ruin everything!"

Seconds after this exchange Ms. Adams strode into the room with renewed vigor. "Well, gang, get out your Arctic projects and polish your presentations. I'm giving you all notice today of when your projects are due in final form and to be presented to the class. You need to practice giving your written report orally over the holiday break. If you don't practice it aloud, it will show in your presentations, believe me! So practice! Practice! Practice!"

Both Michael and Nick seemed relieved to have the focus taken off them and centered on the Social Studies project for a while. Michael wasn't a bit surprised when Ms. Adams informed him that he would be giving his report first on the day after returning from "winter break," as she put it. Michael determined that this bit of subtle punishment would not dim the Christmas celebrations that he and his family were planning, not even for a minute.

Jennifer found herself gazing out the classroom window mesmerized by the sparkling landscape that seemed so drab just a few short weeks ago. Suddenly she found herself fantasizing about the Junior League Skating Finals at the Civic Center tomorrow. In the daydream Jennifer skated like the wind with all the grace of a snowflake spinning and twirling and lifting into the air with weightless brilliance. The applause was thunderous and seemed to match the pounding of her heart.

"You look pretty focused on something, but it isn't your project on the Eskimos. Tell us one intriguing thing you've learned today, Jennifer, during this study hour," the sound of Ms. Adams voice made Jennifer fall from her dream world like a heavy icicle crashing to the ground.

"Oh, Ms. Adams...I...ER...I guess I wasn't thinking about the Eskimos but I do know that they have a great party on that first day they see the sun rise above the horizon after the long Arctic night. All the kids come out from their classrooms to see it happen, and they sing to the sun. I think that's kinda cute! It won't happen for another couple of months yet, but I bet they are looking forward to it!"

Ms. Adams was disarmed and intrigued by the image of all the children and teachers out on the playground singing to a long lost sun. "That's a charming thought, Jennifer, I hope you work it into a poem or song or a picture for your presentation! Very, very good Jennifer!"

Jennifer always had that special ability to turn a situation that could be upsetting or confrontational into something lighthearted and funny. It was part of her natural charisma, and the reason Fawn envied her so much. As most of the class turned loving eyes toward Jennifer, Fawn grew more and more anxious to share her magic brew. Fawn thought Jennifer had the charm of a goddess, and all that Fawn desired would soon be infused into her own frail body. "That is if Nick really does have that potent ingredient he was bragging about earlier. He'd better or I'll do everything in my power to turn him into a warty worm!" The thought of Nick as a night crawler afflicted with warts made Fawn giggle out loud.

"Well, well, Ms. Wainwright, you seem amused with Jennifer's project. Maybe you could share a treasured bit from your own. What was it, a project on icebergs? Fawn, who had been pale all morning from lack of sleep suddenly felt the blood rise to tinge her cheeks pink with embarrassment. She felt a sudden surge of anger toward Ms. Adams, whom she thought was "on our side!"

Fawn spoke softly with a note of fatigue in her voice, "Well, I'll tell you this, icebergs are not what they appear to be 95 percent of their size and volume is hidden beneath the ocean. That's how the Titanic got sunk. The danger was unseen, lurking below the surface!"

Benedict whispered to Michael, "What prophetic words! The danger here is unseen, the evil that endangers all of you is lurking below the surface of the everyday routine in this room. The occult influence sifts in innocently in the books read, the games played the movies watched!" Michael reflected, "No kidding! I remember that the Titanic took a while to sink and many people were really out of it. They just kept eating, drinking and partying like everything was like normal or something. I think that's just like us right here, right now!"

Ms Adams broke into Michael's revelatory thoughts with a pithy comment, "That's why we have the saying, or colloquialism, "That's just the tip of the iceberg!" Anyone ever hear that used?

"Yep," responded Sylvia cheerfully, "that's what my mother says every time I clean out a bag of trash from my room!" The class erupted in loud guffaws and Sylvia joined them in laughing heartily at her own foibles. Sylvia was genuinely good hearted, but somewhat of a slob. Even her locker at school spilled out onto the floor with an abundance of books, papers, animal posters, stuffed dogs, bears and piglets as well as an odd assortment of brightly colored scarves, hats and mittens, that remained until the very last day of school. Traditionally Sylvia wore several of the hats home on that last day of school, in the heat of June, just for comical effect.

Sylvia's quirky personality attracted a fond response, especially from the boys in the class who treated her with respect and included her in their adventures. This was unusual for a girl in fifth grade, especially at G.W. Fawn was looking forward to having Sylvia as part of her circle of friends. All morning in her imagination Fawn drew from Jennifer's source of popularity with eagerness that bordered on lust. Twin spirits of jealousy and witchcraft danced about Fawn's head making it nearly spin with false hope and desire. Fawn felt faint from exhaustion and emotion and experienced a thrill of delight when the recess bell finally rang half way through a boring drill on the multiplication tables.

"What does she think, that we're babies with this multiplication drill stuff?" Nick muttered under his breath. "Meet me outside, Fawn, and bring your friends with you!" Nick grabbed his leather jacket and went out the side door onto the freshly plowed playground.

Fawn responded by grabbing three of her best friends, Sarah, Rosemary and Jasper and pulling them over to the side of the room where they bent their heads together to listen intently to Fawn's plan. "Ingenious! But how are you going to get Jennifer to swallow the potion?" Rosemary queried. Black bangs framed her face and she tugged at them as she spoke.

Jasper, a tall ebony skinned girlfriend from Haiti threw her head back and laughed softly. "Honey, you're not even going to get Jennifer to come within ten feet of you. This I've got to see!"

"I'm sticking around for the whole show, too!" Sally chimed in. Sally and her family were part of Fawn's coven, so they had known each other for years, since they were toddlers, really. "My money is on you, Moonbeam. You go, girl! You've got some powerful spirits on your side and I'm wagering you'll pull it off!" Sally was one of the inner circle of close friends who always referred to Fawn as Moonbeam.

"How much?" Jasper asked half seriously.

"You want to bet ten bucks on it? I've got some extra spending money now that I've finished my holiday shopping," Sally retorted. Fawn looked gratefully at Sally for her extravagant vote of confidence.

"Okay, I'm willing to put my money where my mouth is," Jasper agreed while checking out the contents of her wallet. "Yep, it's a deal!" she responded confidently.

"Don't count me in on this bet," Rosemary whined, "I haven't got enough in my purse to buy a can of Diet Coke! Speaking of which, can anyone lend me a dollar?"

"I will at lunch," replied Sally, "if I win all the sodas are on me! Come on Fawn; let's get out for a breath of frozen air. I can't believe they're making us go outside in this weather!"

While this conversation was going on at the side of the room, Ms. Adams had called Michael forward for a word in private.

"Michael, I'm giving you a break on this. I spoke with David Charlie, the janitor, this morning and he told me he'd pay twenty bucks to have you hand shovel the small walkway to the teacher's parking lot beside the school. That also includes a small side job of mopping down all the inner staircases at the end of the day. Muddy boots in and out all day make quite a mess. He can do the hallways with the electric floor buffer, but the old guy could use some help. That will give you most of the cash to reimburse me for that owl. I have a feeling you'll be wanting to do that before we leave on holiday break next Tuesday!"

Michael stood there stunned during most of Ms. Adams speech. It sorely troubled him that his teacher still stubbornly denied him the benefit of the doubt about the owl, and now that he knew the truth he wanted to tell her in the worst way. If he did accuse Nick, what would happen? Did Nick still carry that horrid owl in his jacket, or was it hidden somewhere now that Nick knew that Michael knew? Silence filled the gap between Ms. Adam's speech and Michael's response. What should he do?

"Father, give me wisdom to do the right thing." Michael was suddenly aware of Benedict's hand upon his shoulder and felt the prompting of the Spirit to go along with Ms. Adams's plan. He would wait for a clear signal from the Lord to expose the truth. "I'll wait but I need patience, Lord, because I can't stand everyone thinking I'm guilty. I guess it's gotta be your timing on this," Michael uttered softly.

"What did you say, Michael?" Ms. Adams pulled her glasses down the bridge of her nose and peered at him with her penetrating green eyes.

"It's just the right timing to do this," replied Michael, "besides, I like helping ol' David Charlie. I'd do it for free, if I could," Michael grinned warmly and it seemed to break the ice a little between him and Ms. Adams. "That's what I was hoping you'd say. Now go along and get a shovel from the broom closet. You might as well get started on the teacher's walkway right away. You never know, someone might want to get in or out of the school from that lot earlier than dismissal time!" Michael obliged by grabbing his snow parka and exiting the room just ahead of Fawn and her bevy.

Fawn looked and felt like a queen bee with the other girls buzzing about her now infamous plot. "Well, I for one would love for someone to take Miss Popularity down a peg or two," Rosemary sneered. She felt compelled to gossip about everyone she knew. "I hear she's got her heart set on winning the Junior Skating Championship tomorrow and that several of her so called friends aren't rooting for her to win. She's stuck up enough already!" The small green demon circling her head chuckled at this thought and drooled on Rosemary's head.

"Wouldn't it be marvelous, darling, if all that skating talent transferred to you!" Sally spoke with the air of adult sophistication and could be quite funny when she got into her, "Dahhling," routines. She was very adept at mimicking some of the adults in their coven circle and could "do" a perfect Clarice Brimmer who had ties to the Salem and Gloucester covens of Massachusetts. Michael glancing over at the girls saw both Sally and Fawn had large demons of the occult trudging along beside them. Although they couldn't see it, both girls wore ankle chains that connected them to these evil creatures. The pale wraith of the potion also whirred along overhead on gossamer wings. She had "fairy" like qualities and was deceptively pretty this morning. Of course, this was a disguise for the wicked beast that lay underneath. The fragile "costume" it had assumed was acquired to lure Fawn into the trap of believing all was done in the name of white witchcraft.

"This won't hurt Jennifer a bit, not one bit. And she'll enjoy being part of my entourage. I may even let her be my best friend, who knows?" Fawn had rationalized the act. "It can't hurt her to share some of her gifts and talents with me, after all. Isn't that what her so-called religion is all about? Sharing?" Fawn was thinking all these deliciously self-centered thoughts when she nearly bumped into Nick who was waiting for her at the side door of the school.

"Come over here, girls, and see what my power powder can do to energize this brew of yours!" Nick boasted in a rather loud voice. Standing not three feet behind him was Michael with his shovel in hand, working to dig out the footpath for the G.W. faculty. Michael was horrified by the convergence of evil spirits over the group of girls now banding together to see what Nick had to offer. Michael

127

was also aware of his own unique vantage point. For the last fifteen minutes he had energetically shoveled the short pathway clear, starting at the parking lot and was now standing a few feet from the side of the playground and side door to G.W. Michael, because of his obedience, was uniquely positioned to see and hear the proceedings. He was very aware of the protection afforded by the whole armor of God. It was as if he were almost invisible to the group intent on fixing this "brew," belonging to Fawn.

"The glory of God is on you, Michael, protecting you. They are not aware of your presence here, but you must watch what takes place carefully so that you can witness to the truth and act to protect and defend God's warriors," Michael could hear Benedict's voice clearly and he turned to catch the image of the angel standing beside him. As he looked at his guardian Michael slowly became aware of the powerful Sword of the Spirit at his side. He rested his hand upon the hilt, ready to use it if the occasion warranted his immediate intervention.

Nick stuck his right hand into his jacket pocket and withdrew three white packets, which he proceeded to rip open. "Hey, you Guys! Attention! Watch the Power Powder mix with this brew so that it will act and do what you want it to do!" Nick flourished his hand waving it repeatedly and ceremoniously over the open mouth of the thermos and finally in the hushed awe that the group reverently gave him, emptied the potent packets one by one into the steaming liquid."

Michael almost burst out laughing. This was no "Power Powder," being poured into Fawn's thermos, it was the three packets of sugar Nick had grabbed earlier that morning at Sally's Bakery.

"Benedict, what is this? A joke?" Michael whispered to the attentive angel at his side.

"Shhh! This is very important for you to see and discern. Pay attention quietly. It is all part of God's plan." Michael was sufficiently embarrassed and grew quiet again as he watched different "magical words" and posturing take place over the thermos. He caught the intent of the potion from what was being said, and a holy anger rose in him. How could they dare to plot against his friend Jennifer in this way! He almost lunged at the group of them, but was held back in gentle restraint by Benedict.

The group dispersed and Michael watched as Fawn sauntered toward Jennifer looking for all the world like the wicked witch in Snow White as she approached the innocent girl with the poisoned apple. Michael followed and stood closely enough to see Fawn open the thermos and pour the golden colored liquid into the lid until it brimmed full and sent a waft of steam into the frigid air.

"Hey Jennifer, how are you doing?" Fawn greeted her in a sweet tone.

"I'm fine, Fawn. I'm just sitting here relaxing a little with Kerry and Silvia. Got a big day tomorrow!" Jennifer was uncomfortable around Fawn, but it was not in her nature to be unkind or unfriendly.

"You must be feeling pretty nervous with the big competition coming up!" Fawn spoke soothingly and with surprising compassion in her voice.

"Well...yes, I have to admit I am pretty nervous, but being uptight and anxious won't help me one bit. As a matter of fact it will probably make my performance look a little off. The routine won't flow if I don't relax and go with it." Jennifer was surprised that she was sharing so much of her inner turmoil with this strange girl.

"Listen, I have just the thing to help you relax. I made some awesome honey chamomile tea this morning. Why don't we share what I have? I've got an extra mug right here in my lunch bag." Fawn reached into her brown paper sack and withdrew a lovely pink mug that featured famous images of Degas' ballerinas around the circumference. She filled the mug with more of the golden liquid.

Michael stood a few feet away from the proceedings with his shovel in hand. He was at first mesmerized by the proceedings. He could see the white faced wraith of an evil spirit hovering above both girls. It had the gray eyes of a wolf and the sharp fangs of one too! He was aware of Jennifer's guardian angel who took a defensive stand with the shield of faith in front of her charge. Jennifer took the mug offered to her and Fawn said a cheerful, "Here's to you and me!" clinking the cups together in a salute. Fawn lifted the mug to her smiling lips and took several big gulps in her enthusiasm.

CHAPTER 15

To Michael everyone seemed to be moving in slow motion. Benedict shoved Michael forward saying, "NOW, Michael. It's time to defend!" Michael lurched forward and knocked the cup from Jennifer's hand as it was being raised to her lips. Jennifer's angel, who had been praying quite loudly, raised her arm to salute Benedict and Michael.

The golden liquid splattered all over the pristine snow bank in back of the girls. The pattern it made on the snow looked like a twisted serpent, long and golden in color like an exotic tropical snake. The pink ballerina mug shattered on the ground, lying in several big shards.

"Look at what you've done, you clumsy oaf! What on earth did you do that for?" Fawn screamed.

"No, I did it for a heavenly reason, not an earthly one, Fawn!" Michael retorted. Everyone in the group stood with mouths gaping open, in utter shock of the drama of the moment.

Suddenly Fawn's face grew ashen white and she collapsed onto the ground. Michael rushed to her side and began praying for her, that God would be merciful to her and forgive her for what she was attempting to do. "Father, if there was anything harmful in that brew, please save Fawn from it. Do not let the enemy win today, Father! I ask this in Jesus' mighty name!" Michael prayed fervently. Ironically, it was Jennifer's angel who grew bright with this prayer and took it as if it were a fragrant gift in her arms. With wings spread wide, the angel ascended to the throne room of God carrying this first petition on behalf of Fawn. Others were too stunned by Fawn's sudden collapse to do or to say much of anything for several minutes.

Finally Frank, Michael's friend, caught on to what had just happened and rushed to the interior of the school to get Kathy Ames, the school nurse.

"I can't believe what I'm seeing!" yelled Sally as she turned from the stricken face of her friend. She sank down onto the snow bank beside the serpentine design melted into the snow. "What does all this mean?" she moaned. Michael took off his jacket and placed it under Fawn's head. Despite the chilly winter air, Michael felt quite warm as the healing power of the Holy Spirit flowed through him as never before. Michael felt God's presence strongly and knew that there would be more for him to do shortly.

Kathy Ames came running from the school with only her Irish fisherman's sweater around her. She looked flush in the face despite the cold. "Here, back away, children. Give Fawn space to breath." Kathy knelt beside the fallen girl, taking her pulse and feeling the clammy skin under her fingers. "Michael, run in and call 911! Get an ambulance to this school quick!" "Dear Lord, what happened here? Did this girl take something...a pill or drugs of some kind?" Kathy looked up from the stricken Fawn and directed the urgent question to the students closest to the fallen girl.

Everyone who had been out on the playground now ringed the original circle of girls: the fourth, fifth and sixth grades plus two recess teachers, including the gym teacher. She and Ms. Adams had been on duty and felt horrified that something so serious had taken place on their watch. They had been discussing holiday plans together and in truth had missed the initial incident all together.

"Was Michael involved in any of this?" Ms. Adams asked sharply.

"Yes, but only in saving Jennifer from drinking whatever Fawn just took!" Sally explained.

"What do you mean what Fawn just took?" Ms. Adams and Ms. Ames shouted together. After the briefest of pauses, Sally came out with the whole potion plan and how Fawn had gotten the idea from the Chad Charmer book.

"How did Michael know to knock it out of Jennifer's hand, then?" Ms. Adams asked suspiciously.

"Because he must have seen the powder that Nick added to the brew...honestly...Fawn told us it was mostly just tea and honey and some herbs and spices and like that!" Rosemary blurted in near hysteria. "You poisoned her Nick! It was you with that power powder you added!" Rosemary accused Nick loudly and every head turned in his direction. Nick, on hearing this began to back away from the group and turned to run toward the gate. Frank sped after him and neatly tackled Nick to the ground.

"I didn't do nothin'! That powder was just pretend!" Nick bawled. Nick stood up brushing snow and debris from his jacket. Jasper raced over to confront Nick and to be sure he didn't try to escape.

"Then why is Fawn lying here dying?" screamed Jasper right into Nick's face. Nick began to cry, big loud sobs racking his body.

"Back away children! Here come the medics. They'll take Fawn to the hospital and make her right. You'll see!" Ms. Ames tried to calm the group and get them to open up the circle. The red flashing lights of the ambulance signaled distress to everyone passing by on the street. Adults from the town now joined the crowd of children and teachers surrounding the schoolyard drama.

Mr. Gladstone saw the emergency light reflected in his office window. He leapt from his leather chair scattering financial reports onto the floor. He flew from the office and bounded down the steps and out the front door. With solemn authority the principal began wading through the crowd of onlookers until he got to the center of the situation. Just as he approached, the medics jogged down the shoveled path to the girl stretched out on the ground like the victim of some awful crime.

Fawn turned her head to the side and vomited some golden liquid into the snow. Her eyes fluttered open for an instant, then she closed them again, unconscious once more.

"Fawn, Fawn, dear...what did you put in that potion of yours? Please wake up Fawn dear, and tell us!" Ms. Ames voice was calm, yet commanding. Fawn remained still and unresponsive.

"Mr. Gladstone, I'm going to ride in the ambulance to Hawthorne Hospital. Ms. Adams will fill you in on what has just happened. Don't be too hard on the boy, Nick. We don't know what has happened yet," said Kathy Ames. She then turned toward Fawn and began praying silently under her breath as the two strong armed medics lifted her limp figure onto the stretcher. The nurse had laid a hand on Fawn's chest as the stretcher was hoisted between the two men. Clutched in Ms. Ames other hand was the thermos with whatever poisonous liquid residual remained as evidence of the ingredient that worked such a potent effect on Fawn. Kathy Ames intended to bring the thermos directly to the hospital lab, but for right now the most powerful help she could give was the loving prayers of a faithful intercessor. The group traveled swiftly to the open doors of the waiting emergency vehicle. Everyone stood in stone cold silence until the doors of the ambulance slammed shut and the flashing beacons of the vehicle disappeared onto Main Street.

The eruption of the siren's wail matched the eruption of noise and confusion on the playground. Ms. Larch, the gym teacher, was ordered by Mr. Gladstone to ring the recess bell and get the classes of students under control, in line and into the building where some reason would prevail and things would be sorted out. Parents who had come in from the street were frantically demanding to know what had just happened and if their child was involved in any way. Mr. Gladstone said that to his knowledge only one student was involved with the situation, and that he needed to return to his office to inform the parents that their daughter had just been taken to the hospital.

As the teachers organized the students and led them back into the building, the crowd dispersed. Mr. Gladstone got a quick update from Ms. Adams as to what had happened and an assessment as to blame.

"Come with me, young man, we have things to discuss in my office," Mr. Gladstone took Nick firmly by the elbow and led him into the side entrance of the building.

Nick, usually defiant in circumstance where the finger of blame was pointed in his direction, melted in fear because of the seriousness of the situation. Fawn could be dying, for all he knew. "Ssssugar...it was just sugar!" was all he could manage to get out.

Jennifer stood shivering in the back of the classroom. She was in shock as she realized that the ambulance could very well have carried two passengers instead of one! She wasn't sure that Fawn was really to blame, after all she had consumed the drink herself...first! "Oh, dear Lord, help us to know the truth in this awful mess and help Fawn recover. Don't let her die, Lord!" Sylvia and Kerry had their arms around Jennifer comforting her and crying with her for the awful event that had just taken place.

"Everyone sit down, please, and let's have a classroom discussion of what has just taken place. I need to make a report to Mr. Gladstone so that he can put things together for the Wainwrights to understand what has happened here today!" Ms. Adams was clearly shaken and although she spoke in a rational organized manner, there was just an edge of hysteria to her voice. Everyone sat down immediately, eager to cooperate, anxious to help Fawn in any way possible.

Meanwhile Michael and Nick faced each other in the principal's office with the stern face of Mr. Gladstone hovering above them. "Nick, I've just gotten a hold of Mr. Wainwright. He's leaving the Shop and Save and heading to the hospital with his wife. Luckily they were together and not far from Hawthorne. We need to know what was in that powder you put in Fawn's thermos and we need to know now!

"Mr. Gladstone, I swear it was sugar, but I can't prove it. I threw away the packets. I just threw them on the ground after I poured out the sugar. I swear it was just sugar!"

"Michael, thank you for racing in here and phoning 911, you may have saved Fawn's life! You may return to your classroom now." Mr. Gladstone put a hand on Michael's shoulder as a gesture of thanks.

"Mr. Gladstone, I need to tell you something that I know about this situation..." as Michael spoke Nick glared angrily at him.

"Go ahead and accuse me! It's your turn now! Go ahead!" Nick spat the words out at Michael. Benedict unsheathed the sword that hung at Michael's side and thrust the Sword of Truth into Michael's hand. Michael drew authority and power from it. He knew in that moment that the truth would win, and that the battle was truly the Lord's.

"Mr. Gladstone, I saw the whole thing! I saw Nick take the sugar packets this morning at Sally's Bakery. We happened to be there this morning before school. It was sugar that he added to Fawn's magic potion or whatever she called it. This had nothing to do with Nick, I'm sure of it. I saw him rip open the same packets he had shoved into his jacket pocket. They were still there in his pocket where he had put them earlier and that's the truth of the situation. Whatever poisoned Fawn...it wasn't anything Nick did, believe me!" The sword of truth flashed brightly in Michael's hand. As he spoke, it slashed through the shroud of hatred surrounding Nick. The light of truth illuminated the darkness of evil conspiracies with its brilliance and grace.

Nick stood in stunned silence. The demon owl that had clung to him shrunk to the size of a pygmy owl and flapped about to keep a toehold on the situation.

Michael's sword of truth flashed brightly, cutting to the heart of the situation and nearly freeing Nick from his hatred and anger. "That's exactly it, Mr. Gladstone. Michael saw it all!" Nick spoke calmly for the first time since he had been accused and he gave Michael a momentary look that expressed relief, surprise and even admiration. "What kind of guy would help his sworn enemy like that?" Nick wondered almost aloud.

"Michael, that's very generous of you to stick up for Nick. I believe you since you, of all people, have nothing to gain by helping Nick out of this...this mess! Both you boys return to Ms. Adams class. I'll let you all know the minute I hear from the hospital! Nick, stick around and touch base with me at the end of the day," Mr. Gladstone commanded.

Once they stood alone, outside the Main Office door, Nick turned to Michael with a look of amazement on his face, "I don't get it, Michael! Why did you stick up for me in there? It wasn't as if it helped your case any!" Nick's voice quivered with the emotion of the moment.

"That's not what this is all about, Nick, helping my case or yours. It's about telling the truth. I told you that the Truth would set you free this morning, didn't I!" Michael responded in a kind tone.

"Oh, now I get it! This is confession time, is it? Well don't expect me to turn myself in for swiping that owl ornament! Because that's in your dreams, buddy! And don't think you can pin it on me, neither. If I ever had that owl with me, it's well hidden now where you and nobody will ever find it!" Nick broke into a run toward the classroom and entered it with a crash of the door slamming behind him.

Ms. Adams jumped three feet in the air with the noise of Nick's arrival, which was closely followed by Michael's more solemn and quiet one.

"I just got a call from Mr. Gladstone, and he has explained that you verified that the ingredient Nick added to that brew was sugar, and not anything harmful. Is that correct, Michael?" Ms. Adams questioned. For his part Michael just shook his head in the affirmative. He was suddenly weary from the emotions of the battle he had been engaged in with Nick. "We'll just have to wait and see what we hear from the hospital lab to verify this." Ms. Adams was most serious in her tone and expression. The entire class seemed on the verge of booing and hissing when Nick entered the room, but now there was a collective sigh and tensions lightened.

All through Ms. Adams' speech, Nick kept his head and eyes lowered as if stricken with guilt, for indeed he was suffering guilt for the first time in his young life. Strange thoughts were racing through his mind. "Why did Michael tell the truth for me? If I were him I would never have done that...Why? Is telling the truth that big of a deal?" Nick wondered. The horned demon puffed himself up seeing the doubt playing on Nick's features and began whispering negative thoughts. " I bet he's hoping I'll come clean and let him off the hook. Well, that's not going to happen! I'm not takin' the blame. Chad Charmer never took the rap for stealing stuff he needed. I'm not either!" Nick's head was spinning and he could barely tune into the class discussion of the incident.

Meanwhile, Ms. Adams was questioning the class for tidbits of information she could pass along to Mr. Gladstone. It was soon ascertained that Fawn made the brew the night before.

"What was the purpose of this so called brew? Does anyone know?" Ms. Adams queried. The silence from the class was profound. Minutes passed with no one speaking. The silence was finally broken by the sound of jangling bracelets as Jasper raised her arm to answer, "I believe I know! Fawn was hoping to share that potion with Jennifer when Michael knocked it out of Jennifer's hand. I don't know how he knew he should do it! Michael, how did you know that anyhow?" Jasper turned to direct this last bit toward the hero of the moment.

Michael, who had his head resting on folded arms, murmured quietly, "If I told you, you'd never believe it!"

"What was that, Michael?" Ms. Adams was anxious not to miss a detail.

"I said you'd find it hard to believe, but my guardian angel made me do it." Michael spoke with an edge of exhaustion in his voice.

The class erupted in laughter at Michael's answer. Michael looked bemused by it all and didn't take offense at the gleeful attitude of his classmates. He was happy to see people laughing after all the tension and distress that had filled the room.

"Okay, Michael, your angel made you do it. All I can say is thank God you are clumsy, if that's what it was!" Ms. Adams countered.

"Yes, I thank God," Michael replied.

"But why was I supposed to drink that poisonous tea?" Jennifer wailed. "Can't someone answer that question?" Jennifer directed her gaze back at Jasper hoping to get more out of Fawn's friend.

"Well, I'll tell you the truth! Fawn was jealous of you, Jennifer, jealous of your popularity, you and Kerry and Sylvia seem to have it all! She wanted to skate like you, too. She wanted to be friends with you, but just didn't know where to begin. I guess she wanted to *be* you! Fawn was a Jennifer Wannabe!" Jasper concluded this speech with a shake of her pretty head.

Jennifer looked more sorrowful than ever, "I never dreamed that Fawn would want to be like me.... Never! I wish I had paid more attention to her. Maybe if I had been kinder to her this never would have happened," Jennifer moaned.

"Jennifer, that's not true," Maria Gracia spoke up. "You *are* kind to everyone. That's why everyone loves you so much!"

"Don't go on a guilt trip, girl, I'm jus' tellin' you like it is!" Jasper concluded shaking a crimson-tipped finger at her.

"It doesn't make sense to me," Ms. Adams interjected, "What does Fawn's wanting to be like Jennifer have to do with this poisonous brew she was going to share with her?"

"Don't you get it Ms. Adams? You're the one reading Chad Charmer to us. You know all that stuff about magic potions. Well, Fawn was just trying one out. You know the one that is supposed to bind two people together and transfer one person's gifts to the other one. It's not in this book, but in the next one. The spell is called the Potion of Pandora and it's in Chad Charmer's Potion Problems. I think that's the volume after this one," Rosemary blurted all of this out in one breath. Her cornflower blue eyes wide with almost a startled look, shy Rosemary was clearly surprised that she had so much to say on the topic. She went back to pulling on her bangs, a nervous habit she had developed in kindergarten and never outgrew.

Ms. Adams looked physically ill with the realization that the Chad Charmer books could have influenced the tragedy of the day. She jotted every word down in her notebook. "Listen, class, I think we do need to move onto our Science lesson on the remarkable workings of the human brain. Take out your notebooks, we are going to sketch and label the parts of the brain!"

Desktops flipped open and kids started to discuss the Fawn tragedy in hushed tones behind the shield of the raised lids. "Listen, we've got to get this done before lunch, so let's go...NOW!" Ms. Adams fairly shrieked this last word as if it were an expletive. The classroom phone interrupted what could have been an angry tirade on responsibility. "Yes, Mr. Gladstone, I'll send him down to the office immediately!" Ms. Adams responded to the demand issued over the phone.

Nick was shocked to hear his name being called. His eyes followed the length of Ms. Adams' outstretched arm to the fingertip, which pointed to the classroom door. "Go! Mr. Gladstone wants you to report to him at once!" Ms. Adams commanded. Nick slunk to the door and exited in an almost silent fashion, a sharp contrast to his arrival a half-hour earlier.

CHAPTER 16

Leo and Lilith Wainwright sat with hands clasped together on the edge of their seats by their daughter's hospital cot. Leo commented, "It feels like my breath has been sucked right out of my body! Dear God, please help our little Moonbeam recover!" This was an unusual invocation of God's name on the part of the elder Wainwright; usually it was, " by the horned god," or in "Ishtar's name," or by some other pagan goddess of fertility and wisdom. Today the Wainwrights were stripped to their deepest needs and knew instinctively from their childhood backgrounds to Whom they must turn.

"Dear God, please help our little Fawn. We love her so much! God help us!" Lilith gasped. The coven and all its New Age glamour paled in comparison to this great need, desperate hope and the One to whom these prayers were addressed. God in Heaven listened with a tender Heart to the prayer he most frequently hears from his children on earth, "God, help!"

Fawn's pale eyelids fluttered. Her sapphire eyes, eyes that had been so dim with a drugged mist, now shone as she looked upon her parents. "Mom, Dad! What happened? Why are you here?"

"Oh, thank God!" her father gasped. Lilith could only sob and hug her daughter as if she had returned from the dead. Indeed, if truth were known, Fawn nearly had died.

"Oh, my little Fawn, tell us what you put in that deadly brew!

What did you use?" Leo felt the need for urgency in getting information to the medical team that was trying to analyze the toxins: those left in the dregs of the thermos and those in Fawn's bloodstream. "Oh, Daddy, the red berries! I didn't have what I needed. I used the red berries...the centerpiece... in the dining room!" Fawn's strength ebbed as she pronounced the revelations needed to save her life. Her eyelids fluttered and unconsciousness overcame her once again.

Leo's mouth dropped open, for he knew the variety of berries of which Fawn spoke. He had ordered the arrangement himself, never dreaming that the beautiful holiday bouquet would hold deadly splendor for his darling daughter. Leo jumped from his chair, his large frame and powerful movement nearly knocking it to the floor. Before Lilith could even register understanding of the message Fawn had spoken, Leo was communicating with the nursing staff and they, in turn, were on the hot line to the doctors and lab technicians. The key to unlocking the mysterious illness of Fawn Wainwright had been found!

Nick in the meantime found himself trudging slowly to the principal's office, dreading what news he would hear. Nick could almost visualize the headlines in the *Daily Tribune*, "**Young Girl's Tragic Death on the Playground! Evidence Points to Classmate!**" Despite Michael's witnessing to the truth with Mr. Gladstone, all of Nick's fears had resurfaced as he faced the horror of Fawn's fate totally alone. He could almost hear the mocking laughter of the owl demon in his head, "Shut up! You are no friend of mine, are you?" Nick cried. The laughter stopped but the torment of fear like an icy hook still gripped Nick sharply in the pit of his stomach.

Mr. Gladstone was waiting at the door of his office, his somber expression softened by just a hint of a smile.

"Come in, Nick, I thought it would be appropriate if you were the first to hear the news. Mr. Wainwright just called me. Although Fawn is still in intensive care, it looks like she's going to make it. They've just put her through the unpleasant business of pumping her stomach. Seems they've also discovered and confirmed what ingredient had such a poisonous effect on her and it has nothing to do with you, you'll be relieved to know, unless you've begun your own florist business." Nick gave Mr. Gladstone a funny look. He was relieved, but puzzled at the odd comment about being a florist. "What do ya mean, Mr. Gladstone, about the florist stuff?" Nick asked, genuinely curious about the comment.

"Never mind, Nick, I don't think it's in your best interest to tell you what the poison was, but, yes, it was in plant form. You are exonerated. That means you're off the hook. Fawn substituted one ingredient for another, apparently unaware of the deadly nature of the choice she made. I was about to call Ms. Adams to tell her, but I felt that you deserved to find out first. You may return to your class now, Nick. I hope everyone has learned a lesson from this...about the dangers of playing around with potions. Herbs can be dangerous unless you absolutely know what you are doing with them.

"That's what makes me different from Fawn!" Nick mused to himself. "I know what I'm doing! I won't make stupid mistakes. I am a lot like Chad Charmer. I am brilliant in my own strange way, and I'm misunderstood!" As Nick was contemplating his next step in the scheme of things, he had to admit to himself that he was relieved that Fawn was going to live. "I guess I'm not as sinister as most people make me out to be! I do have a soft spot in my heart for ol' Fawn, after all she does look up to me as a sort of mentor. I know a lot more about the Craft than she does, that's evident!"

Nick swaggered back into the classroom just as the interoffice phone rang beside Ms. Adams desk. She leapt to her feet to answer it. "Mr. Gladstone, I'm so glad you've called. What have you heard about our dear Fawn?...Yes....Yes! That's wonderful news! I'll certainly let everyone here know that their concern and positive thoughts have paid off! Thank you, sir!"

"Nick, I understand you were the first one to hear the good news. Fawn will live! She's still under the watchful eyes of the intensive care staff at Hawthorne and they did have to pump her stomach, but fortunately they were able to give her an effective antidote. It seems that Fawn managed to choose berries from a very beautiful but very deadly plant to add to her brew. I guess she thought it would add to the charm of the thing...I don't know. I hope we can prevent any other incident of this kind from happening. I will be making a full report to Mr. Gladstone, complete with all of your comments. Nick, do you have anything to add?" Every head turned toward Nick who sat slouched in his corner of the room.

"Yeah, maybe everyone shouldn't jump to conclusions!" Nick eyed everyone with a sullen anger, especially Frank who had flattened him onto the snowy pavement just a couple of hours ago. Michael turned completely around in his chair and stared directly into Nick's eyes. It wasn't a look of accusation, but it was a direct look challenging him to the truth of the matter between them. Nick lowered his eyes and a scowl spread across his face.

"Nick, you'd better ask someone to give you a hand with the science notes I've just given. We've done some sketching and labeling as well. Best ask someone to lend you their science notebook during lunch break, which I see is just about to happen!"

Michael turned around with his notebook in hand and casually tossed it onto Nick's desk. "Look at that! He's playing right into my hands. I needed something of his, like a notebook, to cast the spell on him tonight! What an idiot! I thought it would be hard to get, and he played right into my hands!" With these calculating thoughts, Nick turned and thanked Michael. He was met by the clear, cool gaze of his adversary, who was by far the most honest, the most giving person Nick had run into in all his born days. Something within Nick revolted at the thought of returning evil for good. It was just a flicker of conscience stirring within his heart. Michael recognized the small signs of a change within Nick and he prayed that the grace of God would fan this small ember of decency into a flame before too long!

Lunch and the ensuing break were unusually subdued. A fine-grained snow began to fall just as the classes filed back inside the building. "Jennifer, I hope the weather doesn't get nasty enough to cancel the competition for tomorrow," Sylvia looked contrite the moment these words left her mouth.

"As if Jennifer needs one more thing to worry about!" Maria Gracia rebuked her friend. Sylvia's eyes began to fill up with tears.

"Maria, you've made Sylvia cry. She didn't mean to say anything to upset Jennifer, but now you've hurt her feelings!" Kerry jumped into the fray.

"Stop it this minute, you guys!" Michael had come up behind them and had ascertained that the cause of the squabble was not anger with one another, but another rotten attack from the enemy. "The enemy wants you to fight with one another so that there will be trouble talking to one another, let alone praying with each other! Don't give in to this attack!" Michael stood firmly behind the group of girls. He moved into their circle and laid his hands on Jennifer and Sylvia's shoulders in a big brotherly fashion. "Let's get going with the counter attack! Michael prayed aloud, "Right now, in the Father's presence, we agree that Fawn will recover totally from this poison. She will know the truth. These occult games are sick! Set her free, Lord! Let her know that she is somebody... somebody we all care about. Truth is she doesn't have to be anyone else to be popular! In Jesus' name, Amen!"

Jennifer looked upset still and added to the prayer in a very soft voice, "Father, give me the grace to forgive Fawn...and myself!" She hung her head for a moment as a solitary tear rolled down her cheek. "Guys, I plan on walking over to Hawthorne after school today, if any of you want to join me. Unless my folks object for some reason, I'll be there by 3:30. I feel like praying for Fawn right there with her, and if she'll let me I want to lead her to Jesus!" Michael, Kerry, Sylvia and Maria all gave affirmative answers, pledging to join Jennifer as long as their parents gave permission. "Will you let Raffi and Bobby know, too?" Jennifer asked with just a trace of sadness clinging to her voice.

"You bet, Jen. You can count on all our prayer support, whether we're there or not!" Michael returned to his desk with new thoughts spinning through his head. He began to plan what he might say to Fawn to get her interested in knowing about Jesus. He was pretty sure that her exposure to Christianity was slim, if it existed at all.

Benedict couldn't read Michael's thoughts, but was sensitive to the conversation he had witnessed and guessed at what Michael was considering. Never one to miss adding advice, Benedict whispered softly into Michael's ear, "The only way that girl has met Jesus is through her interaction with any of you, because the Spirit of the Lord lives within you. That's the only time she has had any contact with Him, Michael! You all have to show her the Jesus in you through the kindness and compassion you show her now, even though some of your group may not think she deserves it!"

Benedict swung around and looked at Bobby as he said these words. Michael knew that Bobby would be the hardest one to convince.

CHAPTER 17

S now clotted on the evergreen boughs of the cedars lining the walkway into Hawthorne Hospital. The gardens looked like a huge basket of lumpy sheets and rumpled towels from the hospital laundry. The Wainwrights sat in vigil at their daughter's bedside staring out onto the white linen landscape from the second floor private room. Each parent seemed wrapped in silent thoughts, regrets and prayers. Each kept within their hearts words unspoken. Late in the afternoon, as the gray sky turned lavender and the fine grained snow grew in size, Fawn opened her eyes wide and gasped, "Where am I? Mom? Dad? What happened?"

Relief flooded Lilith and Leo's hearts. They were both exhausted from the inner turmoil of worry and guilt. Lilith fought back unshed tears of anxiety for what had almost happened and tears of gratitude for the fate Fawn had narrowly escaped.

"You drank a dreadful brew, Fawn. Do you remember the brew you made and drank? It was in your thermos. The doctors confirmed it was those berries you used." Leo's voice trailed to a stop as a shudder passed through his body. He once again thought of how he had almost lost his most precious daughter.

"Oh, dad...mom...I am so sorry...it was my own stupid fault!" Fawn began to sob for she realized the seriousness of her mistake as she began to take in the hospital surroundings. "I'm at Hawthorne, aren't I? Somehow I remember the awful sound of a siren in the background. I must have come by ambulance! Oh my god! Is Jennifer all right? Have I killed her?"

"No, darling, Jennifer is just fine. She never drank the brew." Lilith squeezed Fawn's hand tightly. It felt so small and cold in her hand, like a tiny fluttering bird that had been caught and nearly frozen in the snowstorm.

"That's right! I was mad at Michael for knocking it out of Jennifer's hand. How did Michael know, I wonder?" Fawn was looking exhausted from the effort of concentrating and conversing.

"Don't worry about anything now. Just get some rest, my darling," Lilith stroked her daughter's brow gently.

"Fawn, I hope you realize that we have pledged in our little coven, to harm no one by our magic. You are not supposed to cast spells on others without their permission. What has happened here was a grave mistake. I hope we have all learned from it!" Leo added. Lilith looked at her husband with barely concealed anger and raised one finger to her lips to insist on silence. "All that can wait. Fawn, I want you to rest now. Sleep if you can. We are staying the night right here by your side. Dad and I have ordered cots!" Lilith spoke comfortingly. Fawn closed her eyes without further urging. Her eyelids looked like two oval opals, pale and luminous in the twilight of the day.

The afternoon went by without special incident in Ms. Adams' class. A video on the workings of the brain was the high point of the afternoon. Ms. Adams had to handle both groups during Literature and English due to the emergency that engulfed Mr. Gladstone and the Main Office staff. The final hours of class were given over to silent reading of The Charmer series or <u>The Lion, The Witch and The Wardrobe</u>. Extra points from book club sales had been used by Ms. Adams to purchase two dozen Charmer books in soft cover.

"I want you to write about the use of animals in these fantasy stories. How are they symbolic? What does the owl stand for in the Charmer book? What does the Lion stand for in the C.S. Lewis book? I want at least three good paragraphs on this," Ms. Adams stated emphatically. The owl demon became puffed up at the sound of its name, but when the Lion was mentioned, a heavenly light engulfed the young warriors and surrounded them with a warm, comforting sense of the presence of Christ, Himself.

At the end of the day, Michael found himself quite alone. Bobby stopped by Michael's locker briefly to say that he would be in touch sometime over the weekend. Michael asked him if he would be meeting the others at Hawthorne later in the afternoon and Bobby replied, "When hell freezes over! Fawn nearly killed my sister. She can stew in her own brew for all I care!"

Michael was about to retort, "Jesus asks us to pray for our enemies and to bless them that curse us!" But David Charlie, the janitor, knocked the words out of him. He stumbled into Michael and both of them slammed into the lockers.

As soon as they caught their breath, David Charlie launched into a tirade, "Look at that! The floor is coated with icy mud. I can hardly keep my footing indoors, let alone outside. Listen, Michael, I've got to spread some salt on the steps and stairways outside. That snow's been fallin' since early afternoon and it's really made everything as slick as a skating rink! Grab a mop, son, and start workin' on the indoor stairs before one of them teachers breaks her neck tryin' to blow this popcorn stand!" For some odd reason David Charlie always referred to G.W. as "this popcorn stand," and the sound of it made Michael smile for the first time that day.

Michael opened the broom closet wide and jumped a foot in surprise. There stood Benedict in all his glory, grinning at Michael. In one sinewy hand he clasped a mop, in the other, a galvanized pail.

"Great, some people have got a skeleton in their closet, I've got an angel!" Michael laughed. "Well, are you going to come out and give me a hand, or what!"? Michael teased. Benedict laughed heartily. When angels laugh, it's such a sound full of glory and joy that you feel compelled to laugh with them. The Angel and young man roared with laughter, at nothing in particular and at everything in general. The sound of the joy of the Lord rang down the empty corridors of the school. The demons that lurked in the dark corners shriveled with the sound. Some covered their ears as if the sound pained them. Others ran and hid in the basement of the building until the joy subsided. Michael saw that the laughter was a form of spiritual warfare and it surprised him.

"Haven't you heard that the joy of the Lord is your strength,

Michael? The enemy is mocked by the laughter of God's saints. And God in Heaven laughs right along with us! He knows the end of the story and so do you! God wins! Every time! Amen!" Benedict put the mop in Michael's hand and stood to one side as Michael filled the large bucket with hot water and a little detergent. Once Michael had the sloshing soapy pail lifted from the sink, Benedict gave him a slight nudge toward the staircase by the side entrance of the school.

"So are you gonna help me, or just stand there and watch!" Michael joked with Benedict as he began the chore of swabbing down the steps.

"It's my job to watch, Michael, you forget that, but you're ready for action. You've got my sword right here and ready whenever you need it!" Benedict had no sooner spoken these words than Nick came swaggering around the corner of the upper hallway and jumped down onto the landing just above Michael. The thud of his boots smacking onto the tiled floor caused Michael to stagger backwards a bit. He nearly lost his balance on the staircase but recovered and gasped. After a brief and awkward pause Michael grinned with the good humor and joy that had brimmed over within him just moments before. "Well, you arrived in the nick of time, Nick! Want to help? I know everyone is dying for the privilege of mopping these steps and I could be convinced to share the honor with you!"

"What do ya think you're Tom Sawyer? Gonna trick me into doin' somethin' I don't want to do?" Nick responded quickly.

"Hey, that's pretty good! I didn't know you read Mark Twain. He's my favorite author at least so far." Michael smiled at Nick.

"There's a lot about me that you don't know!" Nick rejoined, "and a lot about you I can't figure out!" Nick nearly smiled, but winced instead when the owl demon dug in its talons.

Michael climbed up a step, and Nick advanced after him. "Like what can't you figure out?" Michael continued, subtly probing Nick's soul.

"Well, like how come you pretend to be so friendly. You should hate me if you believe I stole the owl and set you up. If I were you, I'd be figuring out ways to get even!"

"Jesus told me to pray for you, to be kind to you. He hasn't given up on you, Nick! He still believes in you! Remember, the truth will set you free!" Michael spoke softly, and as he did he became aware that he was using the powerful Sword of the Spirit. Warfare had commenced. Michael could feel it all around him. He felt the electricity in the air and the power of God surrounding him as he spoke to Nick. He began to see the owl demon summoning lesser demons to join him on Nick's shoulder. Michael saw a shriveled green spirit and knew instantly that it was bitterness, and the bright green one was envy.

"That's garbage! Jesus loves me? I don't think so! I am a million miles away from his love!" Nick sneered.

"He loved you even while you were stealing that owl, and framing me as the guilty one," Michael spoke softly and with a kindness that was hard for Nick to grasp. "My guardian angel Benedict and I have known about your theft for a while now. We haven't turned you in. *You* need to do that! And you can, with God's help!" Michael was leaning on the Sword of Truth, and it was his support.

"What's wrong with you, man! You and your angel Benedict. You're delusional! Do you know why I'm here? I'm gonna yank a hunk of your hair right outta your head. Know why I'm gonna do that? To cast a rotten spell on you! To make me top dog in that class, and to put you down into a pit, man. Still love me?" Nick glared at him with inhuman hatred in his eyes, a reflection of the wretched influence to which he was subject.

The owl demon was puffed up and in its moment of triumph, or so it seemed to Michael. Michael lifted his sword once more and spoke clearly and firmly, "Yes, Nick, even knowing what you have planned, Jesus commands me to love you and to pray for your freedom from that evil demon and his buddies. I see him, you know. He's got his hooks into your shoulder!"

"Nick looked startled, realizing for the first time the source of the sharp twinge he was experiencing. He wanted to shake it off! He couldn't believe what Michael was telling him, that he cared about him despite the painful truth, the truth of the evil plan he had hatched, with the help of his "spirit guide." At once, Nick felt horrified by what he was planning for Michael. The conscience he had long sought to stifle spoke to him.

"Michael...I...I...don't know what to think anymore!" The owl spirit, sensing a turn toward the light for Nick, dug in even harder. Nick writhed in pain.

Benedict, angered by the nasty owl demon and its influence over Nick, grabbed hold of the Sword of the Spirit, taking it from Michael's hand, and smacked the demon hard across its chest. It tumbled to the ground and was crushed beneath Benedict's foot. Nick looked dazed and without direction.

"Michael, I can't confess. Ms. Adams would call the cops on me. I've been in trouble before! You've got to take the heat. I can't tell the truth, she'll kill me." Immediately a demon of rage rose up and latched onto Nick's back holding him in a vise like grip.

"Get free of this lie, Nick! I'll go with you to Ms. Adams class. We'll tell her together!" Michael was reaching out his hand to Nick when Nick suddenly screamed, "Like hell we will!"

With the angry response still bitter in his mouth, Nick pushed Michael's outstretched arm away, knocking him off balance on the staircase. Down the flight of ancient stairs Michael tumbled at an awkward angle. There was a sickening thud at the bottom of the steps as Michael whacked his head hard, bone against stone.

CHAPTER 18

Nick screamed, "Someone call 911! Help! Please, God, don't let Michael be dead!" Large tears began to roll down Nick's cheek. The demon on Nick's shoulder shuddered at these signs of repentance and Nick's desperate prayer had caused it to loosen its hold. It was still perched somewhat precariously on Nick's shoulder, but was not looking at all like a victorious enemy agent at the moment.

Ms. Adams was the first one on the scene. "What happened? O dear Lord! How could this be?" Ms. Adams slumped down on the floor beside Michael's still pale body. "Nick, go run to the office. Call 911! NOW!" Nick didn't have to be asked twice. He flew down the hall top speed and nearly ran into Mr. Gladstone who was just leaving, briefcase in hand.

"Mr. Gladstone! Quick! Call an ambulance! Michael Minotti fell down a flight of stairs." Nick was sobbing again. The Principal blanched white as a ghost and dropped his bag outside the office door. "How bad is it, Nick?"

"He's knocked out cold! He doesn't look good, Mr. Gladstone! Please, do something quick! Ms. Adams says call an ambulance!" Nick pulled himself together enough to speak coherently. "God, I think I've killed him!" Nick began to sob hysterically.

Mr. Gladstone grabbed the nearest phone, which happened to be in the hands of Ms. Smithly, the school secretary. "Go see if Ms. Ames is back in her office, or if she's gone home!" he commanded the small woman behind the desk.

"Now what's happened?" Ms. Smithly responded, moving quickly around office furniture and out the door without waiting for an answer. Nick trailed in her wake, eager to find the school nurse who might give him the good news that Michael would live.

For the second time that day, an ambulance from Hawthorne Hospital sped down icy streets and skidded to a stop beside the walkway that Michael had himself shoveled earlier that day. Mr. Gladstone, meanwhile, was engaged in the unhappy task of locating Michael's parents and letting them know that their son was being taken to the hospital.

Kathy Ames was just locking up the medical cabinet and tidying things up before leaving the school. She was intent on going back to Hawthorne Hospital to visit Fawn before heading home to her cozy little cottage on Town Lake. The Holy Spirit was prompting Kathy to prayer, and His Presence within her began stirring her, sensing an alert to trouble.

Ms. Ames was nearly knocked off her feet by the invasion of Nick and Ms. Smithly into her small office space. "You've gotta come quick!" Nick pleaded, "It's Michael and he's hurt bad!"

Ms. Ames grabbed her stethoscope and emergency bag and headed around the corner and down the hallway. She tried to keep pace with the school secretary and Nick who were now running full tilt toward Ms. Adams and the crumpled figure lying on the floor at the foot of the staircase.

Although none could see, Benedict was also kneeling beside Michael, tears streaming down his cheeks. His giant wings were covering his friend and charge in a protective manner. "Father, I could have prevented that fall. I should have let Michael keep the Sword of the Spirit, not taken it from his hand. He was without its protection and lost his balance. He was doing You proud! It all happened so quickly. Forgive me if I am to blame! Help Michael! Father, turn this to the good, for Michael trusts in You, and he trusts me!"

Like an earthly angel of mercy, Kathy Ames, whispering prayers and gently laying her hand on Michael's chest, walked out to the waiting ambulance and climbed aboard to speed through downtown

Bridgeton to Hawthorne's emergency room. Ms. Ames' own beautiful guardian angel, Rebecca, accompanied Benedict comforting him as they rode down icy streets. "Go to the throne room, Benedict, I'll watch over your charge as well as mine! You have a direct path to Jesus and you need to see Him…so go!" Rebecca gave Benedict just the slightest nudge to underscore her advice.

It was as if the top of the ambulance was removed and no longer existed; so vivid was the golden staircase to heaven immediately above Benedict and Michael. Benedict bowed to Ms. Ames' angel and began a swift ascent to the Presence of God.

Meanwhile, Nick and Ms. Adams were having a heart to heart talk in the hallway of G.W. Benedict, looking over his shoulder, could see a battle raging around Nick and the teacher. From the height of his ascent Benedict commanded a troop of angels to be deployed on behalf of Nick.

"Oh, Lord, do not let Michael's skirmish be in vain. I know that the battle is yours! The Victory is Yours! I plead for Nick! Do not let him continue to be a slave in the enemy's camp. Free him, Lord, and free Ms. Adams as well!"

"Nick, tell me exactly what happened! Were you and Michael fighting on the staircase? Was he threatening you in any way?" Ms. Adams was exhausted and upset, and with the wording of her last question, left the door open for lies and excuses on Nick's behalf.

"Ms. Adams, yes, we were fighting about the owl ornament!" Nick responded. "He….he wanted to return it to you!" Nick felt the words choking him, sticking in his throat.

"I knew it! I knew it! Michael was the culprit and now look at what's happened. It's all backfired on the poor boy!" Ms. Adams spoke with just a hint of compassion in her voice. Although she wanted to be proven right, she also felt badly about what had happened to Michael and was eager to get down to the Main Office to hear any reports Mr. Gladstone might give her on his condition. She began to turn away from Nick when a sob of such grief escaped from his throat that it gave her reason to pause.

Benedict, from the throne room of God, hurled the Sword of the Spirit to earth. It fell directly onto the owl demon, splitting it in half and causing it to fall, shattered, onto the ground. At that instant

Nick cried out, "Ms. Adams, wait...I took the ornament, not Michael. He wanted to go with me to give it back to you, and I refused. I shoved his arm away from me and he lost his balance and fell down the stairs. It's my fault...all my fault!" Now Nick was crying again in earnest.

Ms. Adams grew pale and felt woozy. She could hardly speak, because Nick's admission of guilt made her guilty too. She had unfairly reasoned that Michael was to blame. She had accused him and badgered him into reparation.

"Where is it, Nick? Give it to me, I want to see it!"

Nick reached inside an inner pocket of his leather jacket and produced the owl ornament. It felt strangely icy in his hand and Nick nearly threw it at Ms. Adams. She took it from him and stared at it in disbelief.

"Why, Nick? Why did you do it? I thought you loved the story and the atmospheric things I did to make it come alive for you!" Ms. Adams spoke in total disillusionment, her fingers wrapped around the little idol.

"I wanted to cast a spell on Michael. I thought he was my enemy. He really was my friend and I didn't see it! I didn't want to see it. I thought I was just like Charmer, defeating my enemies with magic. The whole thing stinks!"

Indeed there was a foul odor in the air, of exploding enemy agents, as each truth spoken by Nick caused them to vanish in a vapor of sulfurous smoke.

"You will be punished for this, Nick! I have to tell Mr. Gladstone about your deceit!" Ms. Adams rose to a dignified height, happy to pin the blame for this disaster squarely on Nick's shoulders, deflecting responsibility from herself.

"Well, I guess I'm really nothing like Charmer, Ms. Adams, and maybe I'm glad! This isn't working out like I expected...or like you led us to believe," Nick spoke with a new earnestness in his voice.

"What do you mean by that, Nick?" Ms. Adams voice sounded weary, and she slumped down and sat on the bottom step of the stairwell. "What did I say or teach you that made you think that stealing, lying and pinning the blame on a fellow student would be okay by me?"

"Do you remember in <u>Broomsticks Arise</u> when Chad stole the magic ring, lied to Master Sniveley, his teacher and pinned the blame on his arch rival Ned Malice? You said that whatever worked for Chad was all right. He was the hero, after all and in the book, even when Master Snidely found out about the stolen ring, Chad was congratulated for using it to win the school spelling championship...Remember? He won the golden cauldron for casting the most powerful spell on Malice and causing him to be speechless for two weeks! It's all right if it works out in the end, you said. Don't you remember?" Nick let everything spill out, every one of the untruths that had been spoken in Ms. Adams classroom, all of the lies that had led to this moment in time, in this sad situation filled with treachery and tragic accidents.

Ms. Adams put her head in her hands in the throes of a full-blown migraine. The dull ache that had begun with the stress of Fawn's poisoning had compounded to a pounding pain in her brow. Ms. Adams was beginning to realize her responsibility in the drama that had led to Michael's accident. The terrible realization that she, herself, played a part in the tragedies of the day overwhelmed her.

Mr. Gladstone stood looming over the teacher and pupil hunched on the bottom step together. "Ms. Adams, Nick, I'll want to talk to the both of you on Monday morning, but for right now, I'm heading over to Hawthorne. It seems Michael's condition is pretty serious. The doctor's initial thoughts are that he's got a fractured skull. Michael's parents are both in the emergency room waiting area while Michael gets X-rayed, so I want to join them, to give them support and consolation."

"Mr. Gladstone, I want you to know that Michael is innocent of the theft that occurred earlier this week. We've got our confession from Nick and here is the evidence." Ms. Adams held aloft the shining snowy owl. It had lost its power and its fascination for everyone who now beheld it. The ornament was the sad object of contention, the focal point of a story that lost its fascination for teacher and pupil alike. The demon spirit had departed now, totally defeated by the truth, sent to the pit of hell by Christ.

"Know what? I'm not surprised that Michael is innocent. Something inside me told me so right from the start! Let me see this sought after prize, Ms. Adams!" Mr. Gladstone commanded. The teacher dropped the ornament into the principal's hand and like a piece of slick ice, it slipped from his grip shattering into a thousand glass shards on the floor. Ms. Adams was momentarily stunned speechless by the fate of her ornament.

"So sorry!" Mr. Gladstone mumbled.

Quite surprisingly, Ms. Adams laughed. It seemed a little inappropriate considering Michael's condition, but the shattering of the wizardly owl somehow represented a shattering of her false illusions about the "great work of children's literature," that she had so highly valued in her classroom. Ms. Adams suddenly felt lightheaded and giddy; the pain in her head had gone. "Mr. Gladstone, I'm going with you. I've got an apology to make to the Minotti family. I want to ask Michael's forgiveness as soon as he comes 'round."

"Let me call my Granny. I want to come, too. She'll be expecting me home to shovel her out, but I've got more important business with Michael, first." Nick's tone was more a demand than a request. He felt certain that despite his wrongdoing against Michael, he would be allowed to come along.

For the third time that day the phone was taken from Ms. Smithly's hand. "Never mind explaining. Just let me know when it's safe for me to make a phone call!" Ms. Smithly sniffed. Mr. Gladstone handed the phone to Nick. He made the necessary explanations quickly and hung up in time to leap though the closing office door and follow behind the flapping coattails of his principal.

Mr. Gladstone swung wide the passenger side door of his little green machine, the "Green Hornet," as he referred to his vintage Ford Mustang. "Hop in Nick. You ride with me. I want to hear how the accident happened and how you got involved with stealing that stinking little ornament in the first place. Remind me I owe...no WE owe Ms. Adams the replacement cost. I believe we should go fifty-fifty on responsibility of paying for it. Don't you agree, young man?"

Nick bowed his head for a moment lost in thought then turned to Mr. Gladstone and surprised his principal, "No, Mr. Gladstone, I don't think so! I think I should foot the entire bill. If I hadn't stolen it, you wouldn't have broken it. Not that I have any money saved up, but I'm willing to help David Charlie around the school. I'll do some hard labor until I pay off the thirty bucks to Ms. Adams. What do you think?"

"I think you've grown a whole year wiser in just one hour, Nick, and you're standing taller in my estimation, too! Now fill me in on how this all came about. Spare no detail! It looks like we're stuck in a little downtown traffic and we've got to take it slow because of the slick roads!"

Mr. and Mrs. Minotti sat in the small cubicle "waiting area," just outside the emergency room. Bill and Meghan Minnotti were holding hands their heads bowed low and close to one another. They looked like young lovers whispering to each other, but in truth they were two parents whose hearts were breaking, clinging to each other in the agony of anxiety over Michael's critical condition.

"Dr. Sands said that he was going to send Michael to radiology just to confirm what he already knows; that Michael's skull is fractured and that his brain is in trauma. He thinks he's in a coma. Dear God! Bill, how does he know that without the CAT scan?" whispered Meghan to her husband.

"He is just making an educated guess from experience, Meghan. He doesn't know and we won't know for sure what's going on in Michael's head until the CAT scan is read. Until that time, let's just pray that God will heal Michael and that he won't suffer any long lasting effects from this trauma," Bill spoke softly but with a sorrowful passion in his voice.

"Bill...could he...could he die?" Meghan bit her lip after saying this. She bit so hard that she drew a thin line of blood, which Bill wiped from her lips gently.

"It's in God's hands, Meghan! Let's be still and wait to hear what the doctors have to say. Sands is calling in a specialist. I don't know his name, but I'm sure he'll see us as soon as he's read the CAT scan!" Bill spoke comfortingly to his wife.

Meghan began to pray softly and her husband joined her. They kept repeating, "Jesus, we trust in You...Help our child...Heal him, Jesus! We trust in You! Don't let him die. Make him like new again. Jesus, we trust in You. You are the Divine Physician. We trust in you!" It was a simple prayer straight from the hearts of Michael's parents. Meghan's guardian angel carried it heavenward, while

Bill's guardian angel stayed and comforted both, speaking the Peace of the Lord over them while they waited.

"Bill, I don't understand it, but suddenly I feel peaceful, like Jesus has heard our prayer. I know he's with Michael, holding him while we can't!" Meghan whispered to her husband with just a trace of a smile on her lips. Bill squeezed his wife's hand and nodded his assent. He felt the peace, too, but couldn't understand it. A moment ago his heart was wrung with agony, and now he felt calm, more than calm. He felt hopeful that everything would turn out all right. "Meghan, let's keep praying, okay?" The two closed their eyes and continued to whisper together as their son's life hung in the balance.

CHAPTER 19

Benedict stood in the throne room of God. He knelt in the holy Presence and soaked in the radiance of Glory and Perfect Love. "Benedict," Jesus spoke from the right throne beside His Father, "Why are you bearing guilt? I have not created you for guilt! You are wiser than that. How long have you been in the battlefield, my dear messenger?"

"I have been on earth for all of Michael's life, and for all of Nick's father's life before that, thirty earth years are not long. I had a century sojourn in heaven before that, worshipping at your feet, Lord. You have had me in the battle on earth for nearly four thousand seven hundred years, but I have had many times of rest and refreshment here with You, My Wonderful God. It is a delight to serve you, although humans can be challenging. This young Michael, Lord, is a delight to work with. That is the reason I have come. Unless it is your Will that Michael come home to heaven, may I carry Your healing to him in my wings? It would be my privilege and joy to bring him Your healing, Jesus. I have come to love Michael as dearly as an angel can. That is not to say I love him as much as You do, for You are His Savior, Lord!"

"My answer is yes, Benedict. Yes to Michael's full healing. Let it be done as a miracle. It will be a sign for others to have faith in Me. A great battle has been won on earth because Michael cooperated with my grace. The harm that was done to him, I will turn to good. Receive the gift of healing from my hand, Benedict! Michael will have joy and rest, but will return to the battle on earth, just as you will. In time...in my timing! Now go to him!" Jesus embraced Benedict with great kindness. Benedict's mighty wings began to glow as Jesus pressed his hands against them.

Benedict's descent to earth was faster than the speed of light. At one instant he was kneeling at the feet of Jesus on a sea of shimmering glass, floating on waves of glory.

The next second he was in the small CAT scan lab along with Michael who was stretched out silent and pale as death. The moveable table fed his slight frame forward until he rested partially within the cylinder of the device. Michael was in position for a perfect picture of his injury. In the instant the technician pressed the control button, Benedict covered Michael's entire being with his powerful wings. Benedict held Michael blanketing him in peace. Seconds after the picture had been completed the healing virtue that had filled Benedict's wings flowed out into Michael's body, mending bones, reducing swelling around brain tissue, aligning every cell with the Perfect Word of God issued from heaven.

Dr. Sands, his friend Dr. Whittemore and a puzzled lab technician leaned over the image to study it in more detail. "This is very bizarre. Yes, I see two cranial fractures, here and here. Also some nasty swelling in surrounding tissue...could induce a coma...but what on earth is that image superimposed on this? If I didn't know better, I'd say a giant eagle had flopped down on the boy's head. It looks like wing structure. It's too bizarre for words!" Dr. Whittemore pulled his steel framed glasses down the bridge of his nose. "Take another shot, Lesley. I can't deal with this one!" he ordered.

The lab technician obediently slid Michael's body into the CAT scan machine again. Because he was as still as a statue, she didn't caution him not to move as beams of X-ray light fired and rebounded slicing through layers of bone and brain, capturing a 3-D image of his head. This newer image puzzled the doctors quite a bit more than the first. They studied it carefully as Michael was wheeled back to his small curtained cubicle in the emergency room.

CHAPTER 20

In Fawn's private room at the other end of the emergency ward Jennifer, Kelley, Sylvia, Raffi, Frank, and Maria Gracia stood in a semi-circle at the foot of the hospital bed. Fawn's parents were happy to see the company of young people visiting their daughter.

"Let's go grab a quick bite to eat at the hospital cafeteria, Lilith. Fawn can have a little visit with her friends while we're gone," Leo suggested. Lilith agreed reluctantly to leave Fawn. She was aware that Jennifer had been the intended target of Fawn's brew.

"You can leave, Mr. and Mrs. Wainwright. We'll keep Fawn company until you get back. Don't worry, if Fawn needs anything we'll get the nurse. We know where you are, too," Raffi spoke in a comforting tone that eased both parents.

"I think we need a little coffee break, dear, and a moment alone to talk, too," Leo further encouraged his wife. Both rose from their bedside chairs and left the room without further discussion.

Fawn was wide eyed at the presence of Jennifer and her friends. "Jennifer, I can't believe you're here. I...I'm sorry for what I nearly did to you. I never realized that the brew was poisonous! Please believe me!"

Jennifer put her hand on top of Fawn's in a gesture of friendship. "I do believe you never meant to hurt me, Fawn. Why would you drink that stuff yourself if you knew it was poison?" The rhetorical question hung in the air for a moment. Fawn's eyes glistened with emotion.

"Jennifer, I can't believe you're here. Why are you here? Do you know why I tried to give that brew to you? Do you understand that I was trying to work magic? I was going to steal your gifts, your popularity...or at least try to!" Fawn looked miserable at this admission of jealousy. "If I were you, I'd hate me!"

"You can see that we don't hate you, Fawn! None of us would be here if we did! But explain something to me, please. Why did you want to be like me? You don't need to steal anyone's gifts. You have plenty of your own!" Jennifer spoke with sincerity.

"You are the most popular girl in our school: you and your friends Kelly and Sylvia and Maria. There is something about you. I don't know. It's a kind of confidence, and joy. I've never seen anyone as happy as you and your friends usually are. Even in the midst of trouble you seem...happy. I don't get it." Fawn looked drained by this effort to explain her motivation.

"My confidence comes from my friendship with someone very, very special, Fawn. I feel like I can do all things because of Him. He gives me courage; he gives me my happiness. He's always there to help and comfort me, no matter what. Would you like to get to know Him?" Jennifer asked.

"Is He your friend, too?" Fawn asked pointing to Sylvia. When Sylvia nodded affirmatively, Fawn continued pointing to Maria Gracia, "And yours?"

"He is the One I count on. I don't know how my family survived what they survived to come here to this country. It was only through His help!" Maria spoke kindly.

"Raffi, do you know this Person they are talking about?" Fawn was growing inquisitive despite her exhaustion.

"Yes, Fawn...I know Him, too. I am never lonely or alone because of Him!" Raffi answered.

"That goes for me, too," Frank added, "Although I don't talk about Him as much as I ought to, or give Him credit for all He has done for me!"

"Well, yes, I want to meet him. Who is it? Is it the new School Counselor, Mr. Fairburn? He seems like a pretty nice guy, funny, too," Fawn mused.

"No, it's not Mr. Fairburn, although he has been called a Wonderful Counselor, among other things!" Kerry giggled.

"Fawn, it's Jesus! He's the one you see in us when we are joyful. I hope you see Him in us a lot. I think that it's Jesus that you are attracted to and don't even know it!" Jennifer spoke with heart-felt conviction.

"And you are willing to help me get to know Him? I've heard a little about Him, but my folks, they're pretty dedicated to the craft. I don't think they'd be too happy to see their only kid turn Christian. Not that I'm doing that. It's just that I'm curious. You'll do that for me? Don't you hate me for what I've done, or almost done, to you?" Fawn directed most of this to Jennifer, but looked around at the circle of smiling faces and smiled back.

"No, I don't hate you, Fawn. That's why we're here...to say let's start over. When you get back to school, come sit with us at lunch and we'll talk. I want to share what I know about Jesus with you," Jennifer held onto Fawn's hand for a moment longer and then rested her hand on Kerry's shoulder. "Kerry here might even teach you to skate. Maybe we'll start our own version of the Junior Ice Capades!" Kerry laughed in delight at this thought.

"Would you like us to get some soda from the fridge? Can you have some? We can stay and visit for a little bit more, until your folks get back. Say, did you ever hear the story of how Kerry here nearly fell through the frog pond ice and I saved her?" Raffi chimed in with his natural charm.

"I'll get the ginger ale. I've come late, but better late than never," Bobby stuck his head in the doorway.

"Well, it's about time, Mister!" Jennifer walked over to the doorway and socked her brother lightly on the arm. "Come on in and join the party. Fawn is looking better by the moment. Don't you think so guys?"

The circle of friends, that now included Fawn chattered away in the growing dusk until a nurse came in and flicked on a bedside lamp. "You must excuse me. I need to take some vital signs! My, my! Did you get permission for that ginger ale, Miss?" The nurse fixed Fawn with a stern look.

"It tasted so good, and I was very, very thirsty!" Fawn defended herself. "I guess I'm in trouble for the second time today!"

"It's our fault, ma'am!" Bobby blushed as he admitted giving

Fawn the drink. "We didn't realize she wasn't supposed to have anything!

"Well, it's not the end of the world, is it?" The nurse laughed. I think it's done you some good. Your color has improved dramatically. Let's see if your doctor will allow you to have a liquid supper tonight. How does broth and Jell-O sound?"

"If it's strawberry Jell-O, I'll live with it!" Fawn smiled brightly. You guys are the greatest, but I think you should all head home now for your own supper. My folks will be back in a minute or two!" Fawn dismissed her new circle of friends with a wave and an ear-to-ear grin. "I think I've finally found some happiness. Too bad I had to go to the hospital to find it!"

"No, not to find it, but to find Him!" Maria said softly.

"Good bye for now, my friend!"

Sylvia was the last to say good-bye. She opened her backpack and removed a small fluffy stuffed animal. "I know you like cats, Fawn, so I thought I'd give you this fuzzy lil' guy to keep you company. I found him in my locker just this afternoon. There's no tellin' what's in that locker of mine."

Tears formed in Fawn's eyes as she hugged the small white kitten to her chest. "You are too much, Sylvia! All I can say is thanks a million. I hope we can be friends!"

"We already are, I think!" Sylvia grabbed Fawn's hand and gave it a squeeze.

As the group left Fawn shut her eyes. She could feel the nurse working over her, but she felt like she was a million miles away, in a beautiful garden with a white robed man. He had the most gorgeous deep blue eyes, like pools you could swim in...pools of love! He was opening His arms to her as she was walking toward him from what seemed like some distance away. "If I could just reach him everything would be so wonderful!" Fawn thought. Then she slept.

On the other side of the emergency hallway, the Presence of Jesus filled a tiny room with golden glory. Michael, barely aware of his own existence, suddenly was aware of strong arms embracing him. The scent of the heavenly garden was in the air. He opened his eyes to see Jesus looking back at him with such profound love that it made Michael shiver with delight.

"Just rest in my arms, Michael. You will awake soon to see your guardian, Benedict. He has brought my gift of healing to you. He carries it in His wings. I desire to wrap you in my love right now and let you know how proud I am of you, my young warrior! You have used the Sword of the Spirit well, Michael. You have told the truth when it was most difficult. You have loved when it was nearly impossible. Do you realize that you have carried the Victory within you all along, because I am Present always, right in your very spirit and never more than a heartbeat away from you! Never fear that you will be separated from me, my dear friend. Keep your eyes on Me. I am Yours and you are mine! I am the God of the impossible! Remember, Michael, that all things are possible with me! So stay in my armor, which is my Presence. Keep your eyes fixed on me! Remember, I am Your General, little soldier! I will bless you with many, many gifts! The first one is nearly finished for now. You have had the gift of seeing my angels, and seeing those who are waging war against my people. You will see Benedict once more and then not again until you need to see Him! He will always be at your side, Michael, until the day He brings you back to Me. That won't be for quite a while yet. You have much to do for Me!" Michael lay quietly in Jesus' embrace. He felt His strength, he felt His holiness but most of all he felt His love.

Michael awoke to see Benedict's face hovering a few inches from his own. Above him and all around him Michael was aware of a glowing tent of brilliantly white feathers. Each quill was shimmering with golden flecks of glory. Benedict breathed on Michael, and his breath had the scent of the garden of heaven. It smelled like roses, but also of strange and wonderful flowers that he could not even begin to describe. Suddenly Michael remembered that Jesus had told him Benedict would bring the gift of healing in his wings. Warmth began to spread throughout Michael's body. It began with a warm tingling sensation in his head, and then spread like a flood of warm oil down his body to his feet. Michael was aware of currents or waves of electricity passing through him and heard Benedict say, "The Glory of the Lord is upon You. His anointing for healing is filling you, Michael! Receive Jesus' love and healing. Let it flow through your every cell, to every part of your body. Your fractured skull is knit together perfectly, in the Name of Jesus! Your brain is functioning normally, according to the Word of God!" Michael and Benedict hugged each other and thanked the Lord together. Michael was feeling strong enough to sit up on his own.

"Benedict, I saw Jesus just a while ago. He told me you would be there when I woke up but He also told me something sad. I think I will not be seeing you again until I really need you. Benedict, I'll really miss you! Why can't I keep seeing you?" Benedict's smile was warm, but his large brown eyes looked melancholy.

"That is the will of God, Michael. We must obey because it is for our good. You will know I am with you and you will be given the gift of seeing me when you really need to do so, and Michael, with the knack you have for getting into trouble, I think it won't be too long before we're talking like this again, my friend!" Both Michael and Benedict laughed at the thought. "Don't worry. I may even give you something to remember me by...but for right now..."

Michael blinked his eyes and in that instant, before Benedict could even finish his sentence, he had vanished from sight. Michael sat back on his pillow, struck by how lucky he was. How very lucky and blessed to have a friend who was his God and Savior, Jesus and to have a guardian friend like the wonderful angel, Benedict!

CHAPTER 21

Down the corridor in the emergency room lounge Michael's parents waited patiently. Although they felt the comfort of God's presence with them, they felt sorrow in their hearts and an increasing longing to hear that their son would be all right. This longing intensified as the minutes passed without report from the physicians.

Suddenly a tall doctor passed through the ER doors. He had on the green uniform of a surgeon, his mask pulled down from a ruggedly handsome face. Golden curls spilled from his cap and his brown eyes smiled compassionately at Meg and Bill Minotti.

"Have you seen our son? Will you be operating on him?" Meghan cried out, nearly in hysteria. The doctor sat down across from Michael's parents. He was broad shouldered and very strong looking, but they couldn't help but notice a hump on his back. It was a large rounded curve that was very noticeable. Both Meghan and Bill wondered about the gifted surgeon who was so disfigured.

"Hello, are you Michael's parents? I've been with your son. I know that Dr. Sands has expressed concern for Michael's life and has told you that he is possibly in a coma. Let me relieve you of that fear. An earlier scan showed several fractures to Michael's skull with possible signs of edema, or swelling of the tissues surrounding the brain. This condition is no longer true of your son. He is well. I just left him. I will be around if he needs me, but let me assure you of Michael's complete recovery. He'll be as good as new by the morning. Raring to get out of here, I would predict!"

"Oh, dear Lord, thank you! Thank you, Doctor...Doctor..." Bill Minotti glanced down at the enameled nametag that hung from the pocket of the surgical gown. "How can we ever thank you enough, Dr. Benedict!" Bill grasped his hand firmly. Michael's parents collapsed into each other's arms. Meghan sobbed convulsively in relief from all her fears. The shower of tears lasted for only a few seconds then she dried her eyes with the edge of her hand. Bill held her close to him for a few moments longer until he was convinced that Meghan felt calm.

"How could our Michael be in critical condition one moment and well the next?" Bill said as he turned to face the doctor, but he had vanished.

"Dr. Benedict?" Meghan called in a strong voice. "Where is he, Bill? Did you hear him leave? I was under the impression he was still seated here with us. I have a million questions for him!"

The door to the emergency room swung open once more and in strode Dr. Sands. "Mr. and Mrs. Minotti, I want to let you know that your boy will be just fine. I can hardly believe it myself!"

"We know. Dr. Benedict informed us that he would be his old self by the morning. Thank you all so much for your attention to our son. Whatever you've done...it's worked!" Bill Minotti grabbed Dr. Sand's hand and pumped it up and down enthusiastically.

"I've done nothing, quite literally, and who's this Dr. Benedict?" Dr. Sands asked quizzically. He had a perturbed look on his face as if this was not the first strange happening of the afternoon.

"What do you mean, who's Dr. Benedict? He's on the staff here at the hospital, isn't he? He just came from our son's bedside. He told us all about the two scans!"

"Holy cow, this is getting weirder and weirder. If I weren't a man of pure science, I would say that it was a miracle that has healed your son!" Dr. Sand's voice was rising in pitch from excitement and disbelief. It was evident that he was being challenged in trying to explain what was going on with his young patient, Michael. "Look, Michael WAS in critical condition when he got here. We were taking CAT scans to evaluate whether he needed surgery and whether we could even perform surgery safely. I don't know how you found out that I ordered the scan to be retaken. The first one did get messed up in a very odd way. I won't go into that now, but the scan was readable. It did show several fractures in his skull and swelling of surrounding tissue was taking place, of rather a dramatic nature. It was not a good situation, Mr. and Mrs. Minotti. We had to be sure about Michael's condition. We needed another scan, and so one more was taken. When that one was developed there were no fractures to be seen. Further more, no swelling is in evidence. Your son is a picture of health. This is a dramatic change for a ten year old boy who had just been in what I would call a coma!"

"And he's not now...in a coma?" Meghan gasped nearly lifting off her seat in a surge of emotion. Bill reached out and put his arm around her to steady her.

"No, as a matter of fact I've been speaking with him. Seems he's been asking for you and a chap by the name of Nick. Wanted to know if Nick was all right. I told him I guessed so, since *he* was the patient and Nick was not," Dr. Sands spoke now methodically massaging his lightly bearded chin. "He also said he was really hungry and could we order a pizza for him! I think not just yet, but I wouldn't be surprised if he were eating pizza for supper tomorrow night! How amazing!"

"*Dr. Benedict* told us he would be back to his old self by the morning!" Bill restated with great emphasis on the name of Dr. Benedict.

"Look, folks, I've been a Doctor at Hawthorne for fourteen years now and I'm telling you there is *no* Doctor Benedict. I don't blame you for being confused. Could you have seen my friend and colleague, Dr. Whittemore? He was called in to consult on the case, a fine brain surgeon from City Hospital!"

"What does he look like? Tall, blonde, good-looking except for that hump on the top of his shoulders, kinda over his neck?" Bill Minotti was gesturing with his hands indicating a massive lump at the back of his neck.

"Mr. Minotti, Franklin Whittemore is short, dark and wears glasses. I will assure you he has no hump or lump or anything resembling that on his back! There *is* no Doctor Benedict."

"But Doctor Benedict said..."Meghan began to reiterate what she had been told when she was interrupted by a new visitor to their circle.

"Benedict! That's Michael's angel, you know!" Nick spoke out brightly. "I bet that's who's with him right now, healed him too, I bet! I believe it with all my heart! Can Mr. Gladstone and I go see him? We won't stay long. I just want to tell him how sorry I am for the whole thing. It was an accident, but I did push his arm away. He was trying to get me to do the right thing, turn myself in for stealing the owl. He and Benedict knew all along, but they never turned me in. He's quite a guy!" Nick babbled on and on quite happily admitting his guilt. Michael's parents and the doctor looked like they were in shock, mouths wide open and eyes somewhat unfocused and glassy, trying to take in all that was being said, but much of it going unregistered.

Bill, Meghan and Dr. Sands stood up next to Nick and Mr. Gladstone. The principal had entered on the heels of his student and was dripping wet snow all over the shaggy waiting room carpet. "Sorry to be joining you so late. I had a few things to take care of at school, including getting permission for Nick to join me here. I guess we've arrived in time to hear some good news for a change!"

"Yes...good news! Michael will be all right. We're going down the hall to see him now. Stick around Nick. You too, Mr. Gladstone. I have a feeling Michael will want to see you both!" Mr. Minotti turned to leave with his wife supported by his arm when a blast of cold air filled the room. Ms. Adams stood in the foyer looking like a forlorn snow woman.

"How's Michael, Mr. and Mrs. Minotti? I know I'm probably the last person you want to see here, but I had to come to apologize to you."

"It seems like there has been a whole lot of that going around today!" Mr. Gladstone smiled at his teacher to encourage her. He felt just a little sorry for her; she looked so bedraggled and unhappy.

"I blamed your son and it wasn't him! I should have believed him. It was like I was blinded by my own pride...by..by.. I don't know what! Maybe I should resign!" Ms. Adams stood there wringing her hands.

"Now, don't go overboard, Ms. Adams!" Bill Minotti spoke. "Michael will be just fine. We haven't had a chance to see for ourselves yet, but I hear he's asking for Nick and that's got to be a good sign!"

Ms. Adams smiled weakly, but there was gratitude in her heart for Mr. Minotti's forgiving attitude. "I want you folks to know, I went to the Dumpster with the Charmer books. They've caused enough trouble!" Bill Minotti smiled his approval and Principal Gladstone gave Ms. Adams a good old-fashioned high five.

"Way to go! I always knew you had good common sense!" Mr. Gladstone clapped his hands together in warm approval.

Ms. Adams blushed. She wasn't quite sure how Mrs. Minotti felt. Indeed, there was no reaction from Meghan Minotti.

Suddenly Meghan Minotti turned to her husband and said, "The lump! It was the angel's wings tucked under the surgical gown! Don't you see, Bill?" For a moment Michael's parents sat in the hushed awareness of the major miracle that had just occurred, then the stunned silence surrounding them was broken.

"Oh, my Gosh!" Bill Minotti's mouth dropped open, "Do you really think Dr. Benedict is Michael's angel Benedict? We thought he was crazy, seeing things that weren't real! Meghan, we saw him, too!"

Bill began to laugh, then Meghan. Nick threw back his head and roared with laughter. "Didn't I say so? Of course it was that ol' angel, Benedict!" Nick gasped between bursts of laughter. Mr. Gladstone, Ms. Adams and Dr. Sands didn't get the joke and they weren't quite sure why, but the laughter was so contagious that they found themselves chuckling too.

Benedict, invisibly present blessed them saying, "The joy of the Lord will be your strength!"

From down the hall they could hear the mirthful sound of belly laughter from Michael. "What are you all waiting for?" he called. With barely time for the taking of another breath, everyone heard a gleeful peal of Michael's laughter, "Man, these things really tickle! Come see what Benedict left behind!"

"For our struggle is not against flesh and blood, but against the rulers, the authorities, against powers of this dark world and against the spiritual forces of evil in heavenly realms." Ephesians 6:12

Printed in the United States
22691LVS00005B/88-306

9 781594 677250